DEATH ON THE TABLE

The man carried into casualty was a Polish seaman—an emergency—in urgent need of an abdominal operation. Four hours later, on the operating table, he died 'accidentally'. From then on the 'accidents' began to occur more frequently ... more violently ... Accidents in the theatre, in the pharmacy, in the grounds of the hospital. And finally every member of medical staff, from the Consultant to the orderly, found himself under suspicion of murder ...

DEATH ON
THE TABLE

Claire Rayner

CHIVERS LARGE PRINT
BATH

British Library Cataloguing in Publication Data available

This Large Print edition published by Chivers Press, Bath, 1996.

Published by arrangement with the author.

U.K. Hardcover ISBN 0 7451 4987 1
U.K. Softcover   ISBN 0 7451 4988 X

Photoset, printed and bound in Great Britain by
Redwood Books, Trowbridge, Wiltshire

CHAPTER ONE

Four a.m. The pool of light from the Casualty entrance spilled across the main courtyard, making the consultants' car park look even blacker and filling the dark corner by the transport office with menace. But only the pharmacy cat, stalking arrogantly across the tarmac, moved out there. Above it the main ward block loomed heavily against the cloud-scudding sky, the even pattern of dim windows breaking its façade into a satisfying checkerboard design.

In the private block, the buzzer from room 204 shrilled sharply in the ward office and Staff Nurse Kennedy, who had been sitting huddled in her cape in the low armchair, woke abruptly from an uneasy doze and swore softly before padding along the corridor to see what the wretched man wanted.

He had a pain, and he knew a cup of hot milk would settle it. Please? But Nurse Kennedy plumped up his pillows and tucked him in firmly, pointing out brightly that no, he couldn't have a drink now, since he was having his operation at eight thirty, and that meant nothing by mouth whatsoever. And, no, no drugs either, she was afraid, not until he had his pre-med at seven thirty. He was just to try to go back to sleep, and remember that after

1

the operation his stomach wouldn't bother him any more, seeing he wouldn't have much of it left, would he? With which cold comfort the man in room 204 had to be content.

On the doctors' residential floor, just behind the main ward block, Barnabas Elliot stirred in his sleep and then buried his head more deeply into his pillow as the sounds from the next room indicated that the obstetric registrar had at last completed that difficult high forceps, and was coming to get some sleep in while he could—although it hardly seemed worth going to bed, seeing he'd have to leave it to take an ante-natal clinic at nine a.m.

On the other side of the corridor, Derek Foster lying on his back snored heavily, and dreamed frankly erotic dreams, while next door young John Hickson lay tidily and silently sleeping the sleep of the just, his stethoscope, torch, patella hammer and ophthalmoscope lying neatly arranged on his bedside table. Hickson prided himself on the speed with which he answered any calls the night staff made on him, so much so that when the rather flighty girl on Casualty once said, 'Our young doctors are so handsome and dress so well—and so quickly!' he had genuinely thought she meant it for him; hadn't realised she was making a lewd joke until Derek Foster, with Australian coarseness, pointed it out to him.

Far beyond the main ward block, in the

2

nurses' home, Lucy Beaumont lay sprawled deep in sleep, her curly black hair rumpled against the pillow, looking absurdly young to be anyone as important as a Medical Ward Sister and dreaming of Barney Elliot with a wealth of detail that would have surprised him considerably had he known of it.

Four fifteen a.m. The courtyard seemed to move and slither as an ambulance curled round the sharp corner of the entrance, sending its headlights streaming across the windows of Female Medical (waking senile old Mrs Chester, who immediately set up a thin whining cry that effectively woke the rest of the ward) and stopped in front of Casualty.

The tired Staff Midwife up in private maternity heard it, and wearily wrapped up the last of the new babies after its bath and told the pupil midwife on duty with her that if that was *another* admission she for one wasn't going to do another delivery, and the day people would just have to be called out. There was a limit to what one midwife could do, saddled as she was with a brace of useless pupils.

Staff Nurse Griffiths on the third floor of the private wing heard it too, and wondered if it could possibly be that suspected ectopic Sir Douglas had mentioned to Day Sister, and then huddled into her cape again as a sharp draught whistled under the office door and curled round her ankles.

The main theatre doors must be open again

she thought petulantly. That was the only place that draught ever came from. She'd have a few things to say to the theatre porter next time she saw him. Those theatre people thought the hospital only existed for them, arrogant lot—

Four forty-five a.m. The telephone on Derek Foster's bedside table shrilled insistently, and then again, dragging him irritably from the delectable depths of a sleep full of dreams of that smashing girl on Male Surgical.

He grunted his usual indecipherable noise into the phone, and tried to wake himself properly as he listened to the thin voice of Casualty Staff Nurse clacking at him.

'Can't he wait until morning, Nurse Graham?' he said, his voice a little slurred. 'It can't be that—oh, all *right*. I just wondered if this was a real bill or just another nursing flap—no, I'm—oh—all *right*, I'm sorry! I'll be down in a minute—'

He slid out of bed, pushing his long feet into fur lined slippers, and shrugged his white coat over his pyjamas, shivering a little. The heating in this place is the most inefficient ever created, he thought irritably, even in June, and went out and along the dimly lit corridor with his hands thrust deep into his pockets, his tousled head sunk so far into his shoulders that he looked like a bad tempered penguin.

Casualty was bright and quiet, the light reflecting cheerfully from chrome and glass and racks of instruments and bottles, and it

4

was warm. Faint tendrils of steam rose from the bank of big sterilisers hissing gently against the far wall, and the whole big central area was filled with the heat, making Derek straighten up a little and feel more alert.

The curtains that closed off the far cubicle swished and opened and Night Sister came out, followed by Staff Nurse Graham. Sister nodded sharply at Derek.

'Good morning, Mr Foster!' she said, an edge to her voice. 'I hope you will agree with me that this *is* a true bill and worth getting up for! Nurse Graham, let me know what is decided, will you? There is a bed available in semi-private by the way.' She turned back to Derek.

'I took it upon myself to assume he would have to be admitted for immediate surgery, and since the main theatres are already heavily booked there is no point in putting him in Male Surgical, which is overcrowded anyway, when there's an available NHS bed in the private wing. Anyway, Sir James is the consultant on take-in tonight, and he's operating in the wing in the morning. It is altogether better to arrange things this way. Now, I'm wanted in Maternity, so I'll leave you to Staff Nurse. Good morning!'

And she swished away, her rubber heeled shoes thwacking firmly on the tiled floor.

'Efficient old bag,' muttered Derek, and Nurse Graham giggled softly and said, 'Sorry

5

about that—she came in to the office while I was talking to you, and got highly shirty because you seemed a little unwilling to get up.'

'Well, who wouldn't be? Anyway, what's the story?'

'Patient's a man of about thirty-odd. Acute abdomen, as far as we can tell. Thing is, he's Polish—a sailor. They brought him up from the docks where his ship berthed tonight. There's no interpreter, I'm afraid, so you'll have to manage as best you can. But he's pretty ill—obviously in pain, and with a temp of 101 and a very rapid pulse—hundred and thirty. I've made up some notes—'

The man in the cubicle was lying with his knees drawn up, and a look on his face that was eloquent of sick anxiety. He turned his head sharply as Derek came in, and shrank back a little as the covering blanket was pulled back.

'Nothing to worry about, feller,' Derek said cheerfully. 'Let's just have a look at this belly of yours—'

His hands moved gently over the man's body and the patient winced sharply once or twice as the square-tipped fingers probed and slid over the tense skin. After a while, Derek grunted and straightened up.

'Pretty obvious, isn't it?' he said to Nurse Graham who stood hovering at his side. 'Look at it—as strangulated a hernia as I have seen this many a day. And if we don't release it soon, he'll be in a right mess. Who's on, did she

6

say? Sir James?'

'Mmm. Sister says he's got a list in the morning—um—there's a gestrectomy first, I think, then an appendix, and a couple of odds and ends—hernias, and a varicose vein or two. All private patients.'

Derek looked cheerful. 'Good oh! Then maybe he'll let me do this one. What time is he due to start?'

'Half past eight.'

'Then I could do this feller at half past seven, couldn't I? Night staff could set up, and the day staff take it. Great. I'd better let the old boy know, though. He's liable to get very upstage if I go ahead and act on my own diagnoses. Which is bloody silly when you consider how much money and effort has gone into preparing chaps like me to take the initiative and all that—'

'You talk as much in the small hours as you do all day,' Nurse Graham said dispassionately. 'And I'd like to get this man settled one way or the other. If you put a move on, I'll get some Ovaltine for you before you go back to bed. *If* you do.'

'You're on,' Derek said, grinning at his patient and patting him on the shoulder with what he hoped was a reassuring gesture before going across Casualty to the office, to sit sprawling over Sister's desk while he waited for the night switchboard man to get Sir James Custerson-Weller's home number.

'Do you suppose people are really born with names like that?' he asked.

Nurse Graham shrugged and shook her head.

'I swear surgeons are like actors—make up fancy names for themselves because they look good over a Harley Street address on an envelope.' Derek yawned suddenly. 'I'm tired—I bet the old whatsit'll do his pieces, being woken at this hour. It's his own fault, though. Ought to give junior people like me a bit more leeway, let us use our own initiative and—oh. Good morning, sir. Sorry to wake you at such an unearthly hour, and on such a chilly night, too, but—er, yes, sir.' He listened for a moment, grimacing at Nurse Graham.

'Er, yes, sir. Well, he's a Polish sailor—' Derek launched into an account of the history and findings of his examination, and when he'd finished said in a diffident voice that seemed odd coming from someone so normally ebullient, 'As your list starts at eight thirty I could take this man to your theatre at seven thirty and get him out of the way in plenty of time for you to start, sir—no, sir, I don't think he can wait till the end of the morning. That's why I called you now. He's pretty shocked—yes, sir. In excellent shape otherwise—'

He listened again, and then looked so surprised that Nurse Graham almost giggled aloud at the sight of his face.

'You, sir? But it's only a strangulated hernia,

8

sir. Surely there's no—no, sir, of course. Yes. Yes—anaesthetist—I'll tell him—Elliot. Yes, sir, Om and scop pre-med, and—the list, sir? Just a moment, will you—?'

He covered the mouthpiece with one hand and hissed urgently, 'What did you say was first on? The gastrectomy?'

Nurse Graham nodded, and Derek returned to the phone. 'Partial gastrectomy, sir. Put him second? Very well, I'll fix that—yes, sir. Goo—' and he winced as the phone produced a decisive click.

Graham giggled again. 'Was he livid?'

'Silly old basket. If he doesn't like being woken up he ought to let people do their jobs. Then he could snore his fat head off to his heart's content. Honestly, he really is a louse. Does his pieces at me for waking him, and then says he'll do the man himself, first on the private theatre list. I'll have to tell the ward people, I suppose, to shift the list one patient up—oh, and Night Sister had better know because of the pre-meds. Aw, nuts—' and he produced a few pungent words that made Graham purse her lips in genuine disapproval.

'Shall I tell Mr Jackson, or will you?' she asked.

'Mmm? Why Jackson?'

'He's Resident Surgical Officer—*and* Sir James's registrar. He organises the operating lists. He ought to be told—'

Derek shook his head and produced another

9

of his jaw cracking yawns. 'No, leave him snooze. Bad enough I'm missing my beauty sleep. He'll find out at breakfast—I'll see him then.'

'Well, make sure you do,' Graham warned. 'He can be pretty bloody minded if people forget his status, and all that. You've got to keep him informed of anything to do with the surgical firms, or he raises merry hell—'

'Ah, status, peanuts!' Derek said, and went back across Casualty to the man in the cubicle. 'I much care for status or anything else like it. I'll tell him at breakfast. I've got better things to do than sit around here phoning people to bolster up their own sense of importance. If the old buffer changes the list it's his business, and Jackson knows what he can do if he doesn't like it. Here, give me those notes will you?—and what about that Ovaltine you promised?'

And after making a hopeless attempt to explain to the worried Polish sailor that he was to have an operation, but that it would be perfectly safe since it was to be performed by one of the country's most eminent surgeons, Derek Foster went padding back to bed, clutching the beaker of hot Ovaltine Nurse Graham had provided for him. He'd made a date with her, so even though he hadn't been given the chance to prove his surgical prowess on the Polish hernia, the night hadn't been entirely wasted.

Seven thirty a.m. Derek, inevitably, ignored

10

the insistent tapping on his door, and went back to sleep. Which meant he missed his breakfast and had to report to Outpatients for a clinic in a state of bad temper induced by a badly cut face resulting from too hasty shaving and a coffee-less interior.

But the rest of the resident medical staff breakfasted, John Hickson looking polished and fresh as he read his *Times* (Top People take *The Times*. It only took me half an hour to become a *Times* reader, he often reminded himself smugly) in strong contrast to almost everyone else.

Barney Elliot looked fresh enough, but far from lively. He wouldn't have much to say to anyone until a sizeable breakfast filled his hollows, any more than would Colin Jackson. Not that Jackson ever had much to say to anyone, apart from shop talk. A bad tempered chap, Jackson, Barney thought, as the older man removed the *Telegraph* from Barney's place at the table, as though it belonged to him by right.

Sister Beaumont reported for duty in a sunny mood. She usually was a happy person anyway, but this morning she felt more than usually cheerful. They were doing a retrograde pylogram on Mrs Chester this morning (and maybe she'd be discharged soon? A hopeful thought, that. She did disturb the other patients' sleep so badly) and that meant a light general anaesthetic. Which in turn meant that

Dr Elliot would be coming to the ward. It wouldn't do to let anyone know just how delightful a thought that was—least of all Dr Elliot—but it made her whistle softly between her teeth as she settled herself at her desk to take the report from the night staff.

The man in room 204 greeted the arrival of the day staff with a mixture of relief and anxiety. Of course he'd be better once he'd had his operation. No doubt about it he needed it. Life had been pretty grim lately, what with the complications of the Business (he grinned a little wryly as he thought about the Business that was lucrative enough to make him a private patient) and the general awkwardness of suppliers and all. Suppliers. Yes. He'd have to do something about that man, soon. Getting a bit above himself he was—

He submitted with what grace he could to the ministrations of the rather harassed junior nurse who came to dress him in long woolly socks and a gown, and said with as good a display of calmness as he could manage, 'Well, not long now. Just another hour, eh?'

'A bit longer, I'm afraid, Mr Quayle,' the nurse said, expertly lifting him up in bed to arrange the gown neatly round his buttocks. 'There's an emergency to do before you. Sister says you'll probably go to theatre about nine or so. She'll give you an injection soon. Just you relax now—'

And she went away, leaving Mr Quayle

feeling anything but relaxed.

Eight fifteen a.m. The Staff Nurse in theatre pulled her mask down to dangle comfortably round her chin as she closed the main theatre door behind her. Trolleys, set. Mayo table, ready. Gloves, out. Gown drums, ready. Mentally she ran briskly through the arrangements for the morning's list, and then made for the anaesthetic room to check that everything there was ready for Dr Elliot before going to see whether Sir James had arrived so that she could send for the first patient. Emergencies. An awful nuisance today, seeing it was her half day and she wanted to get off on time, but it couldn't be helped—

Barney Elliot came through the big swing doors, nodding cheerfully to Gellard, the theatre porter, who was checking the oxygen cylinders on the spare anaesthetic machine.

'See the soda lime is fit, will you, Gellard? I'll need it later today for the first big case on this afternoon's list—Good morning Staff Nurse Cooper! I trust I see you in bouncing health? Ready for work? Nothing like one of Sir James's pernicketty gastrectomies to start the day—'

'Morning, Dr Elliot. And we aren't starting with the gastrectomy. There's an emergency hernia on first.'

Barney stopped. 'What? Why doesn't anyone tell me these things? I haven't seen any hernia, or written up a pre-med—'

13

'Mr Foster saw him in Cas this morning early, and phoned Sir James, apparently. Sir James told him to alter the list and to write up the pre-med. Didn't he tell you?'

'He wasn't at breakfast, lazy devil. Though if he was up in the small hours—oh, well, send for the man, will you? I'll have a good look at him in the anaesthetic room. I prefer to write up my own pre-meds, but it's a bit late now—'

And he went across to the anaesthetic room, shrugging off his white coat as he moved. 'Is there a gown ready for me?' he called over his shoulder.

'Mmm. I set up in there last night,' Nurse Cooper said. 'But I haven't unlocked yet. I'll get the key—'

But Barney had already opened the door. 'You're dreaming, sweetheart!' he called cheerfully. 'This door's not locked—'

She followed him into the small anaesthetic room, her forehead creased in surprise.

'That's odd. I remember perfectly well that I locked up last night—'

'You must be in love again,' Barney said, and laughed. 'Never mind. I won't breathe a word to Sister. Get me my sterile tray, there's a good girl, and forget you forgot.'

'I did nothing of the sort!' Cooper said indignantly. 'I *did* lock up. I have to, when I've put out the drugs and all—but look, I *would* be grateful if you didn't mention it to Sister. I mean, she doesn't like us setting up the

14

anaesthetic room overnight, but it does save time in the mornings—'

'Promise. And *now* can I have my patient? Because the old boy'll be a great deal nastier than Sister if he has to waste *his* time because I'm not ready for him.'

'I'll send Gellard for the patient,' she said, and turned to go. 'Mind you, I still think it's odd. I know I locked up properly last night—'

'Oh, *go on*—' Barney said, and went to wash his hands. And Gellard went to collect the Polish sailor, by now feeling a good deal too ill to care whether he had an operation or not, and Sir James arrived in a pomp of grey striped trousers and black jacket, and the junior theatre nurse turned off the steriliser ready to dish up Sister's first lot of instruments.

The day had started.

CHAPTER TWO

As he mixed the pentothal, snapping the slender glass neck of an ampoule of sterile water and squirting the contents into the yellowish powder before drawing the resulting straw coloured fluid into his favourite big syringe, Barney was happy. It was odd how much pleasure there was to be found in anaesthetics. He'd never thought back in his student days that he'd turn into a gas-fight-

15

and-choke man, the label given to anaesthetists by irreverent third year men, but there it was. The speciality fascinated him, and he was good at it.

Another six months here at the Royal and he'd be ready to apply for a junior consultancy in anaesthetics. And that would mean a better income, and all the agreeable possibilities that more money meant. Like a home of his own, for example, instead of living a celibate life in hospital.

And then he remembered the patient he was to deal with on Female Medical later that morning, and felt even more contented. Sister Beaumont provided excellent coffee in her neat ward office, and fifteen minutes spent drinking it in her company was something well worth looking forward to.

Behind him the man on the trolley muttered in the depths of his drug-induced sleep, and the little Junior Ward Nurse who had accompanied him to the theatre leaned over nervously and patted his shoulder.

'Poor man doesn't speak English,' she told Barney, feeling obscurely that she ought to explain why she hadn't spoken to her patient in the approved manner. 'He just mutters at us when we try to explain things to him.'

'Poor feller,' Barney agreed sympathetically. 'Bad enough to have a belly ache like his without it happening where no one speaks your language. Ah, well, the sooner I put him out, the sooner we can deal with his belly ache, hmm? Roll up his sleeve for me, will you? That's it—good girl—'

And the little nurse blushed and obeyed, wishing she were senior enough to work in the theatres all the time, near this nice ugly man who was always so kind to juniors.

As he gently pushed home the plunger of the syringe and dripped the pentothal into the vein in the crook of the elbow, watching his patient's face all the time, Barney felt the draught of warm antiseptic air that meant someone had come through the big swing door behind him. But he didn't look up until all the pentothal had been given, and the airway tube was snugly in place in the patient's lax mouth. Then, as he fixed the anaesthetic mask into place over the face, he raised his eyes.

'Hello, Colin. Ready for me? Won't be long now—'

The older man shook his head without looking up from the folder of notes he had picked up from the foot of the trolley. 'Not yet—Sir James hasn't changed, so I can't scrub up yet. Where's this patient's notes?'

Barney twisted the knobs on the machine, sending the little chrome markers dancing in their tubes as he balanced the supply of oxygen and nitrous oxide. The rubber balloon of the respiration bag on the machine filled, emptied, filled again and then settled to the rhythmic pattern of the patient's breathing.

17

'You've got them there,' he said, and looked up in surprise as Jackson moved swiftly to the other side of the trolley to stand staring down at the patient. 'Why? What's the matter?'

'What the hell is going on? This isn't Quayle! What do you think you're doing?'

'Giving an anaesthetic,' Barney said, crisply. 'It's a habit of mine—'

'Don't be so bloody funny!' Jackson snapped, and his face was blotched red with anger above his mask. 'The first patient on today's list is Quayle, a gastrectomy—'

'I thought *you'd* have known though I only just found out,' Barney said. 'They switched the list for this feller—a strangulated hernia that came in in the small hours. What's the panic?'

'*Who* switched the list without telling me?' Jackson said, his voice high with anger. 'I don't spend my valuable time planning lists so that people can come along and alter them without so much as a by-your-leave! Sir James will—'

'Sir James already knows,' Barney said soothingly. 'Foster diagnosed the case and called Sir James, and apparently the old boy decided to do the job himself. So there's nothing to worry about—'

'Foster. Interfering idiot!'

Barney frowned, and glanced at the nurse beside him, round-eyed with interest at this disagreement between members of the medical staff. This would be something to tell the girls

18

at coffee break.

'I imagine Foster preferred not to wake you unnecessarily in the small hours. I'd call that consideration, not interfering.'

'I should have been told,' Jackson said stubbornly, still staring down at the unconscious patient on the trolley. 'He should have told me at breakfast.'

'Which he missed. Probably because he had a broken night. Oh, look, Colin, do stop fussing. I know Derek's sometimes a bit slaphappy about the details of administration, but he's a good chap, and meant no harm. If I know Derek, he's spitting bullets because he wasn't allowed to do the case himself. He's working for his Fellowship, remember, and—'

'What did you give him?'

'Hmm? This chap? Pentothal, and nitrous oxide. He was pretty shocked on admission, so I want to keep it light. You'll need a good deal of relaxant, I daresay, come to think of it. Those abdominal muscles will be pretty rigid. Nurse—go and tell Nurse Cooper I want her, will you?'

The little nurse went, and Jackson turned to follow her.

'Well, since you've started there's nothing I can do about it, I suppose. But I'll have a good deal to say to Foster when I see him, and so you can warn him if you see him first. I won't have these damned junior housemen taking the law into their own hands—'

19

Barney shrugged, and grinned at Nurse Cooper as she came in with the junior nurse scuttling behind her.

'We're going to have a *lovely* morning, sweetheart. Jackson's in a temper, and Sir James will probably catch the infection, so Gawd 'elp us all. Look, I want to give this man some curare, so get me some sterile water, will you? I want to use a dilute dose.'

'There's some in the rack,' Cooper said, moving over to the drug tray and the little rack of ampoules.

'If there were, I wouldn't be asking you for some now,' Barney said patiently. 'There was only one and I used it for the pentothal. Now do put a move on. All those surgeons need now is to have to wait for me and there'll be all hell let loose. This isn't one of your efficient days, is it?'

'There was some there,' Cooper said sulkily. 'But I'll get some more. And Sir James has started scrubbing, so you'd better put a move on—'

But Sir James wasn't in a temper. Jackson still had a heavy, angry look on what could be seen of his face as he stood facing Sir James across the table and holding retractors and swabs, but the old man himself was in fine form. He flirted heavily with Sister Osgood, who responded with her usual overdone kittenish giggling, which made Barney wink at Cooper, who moved about the theatre fetching

20

and carrying instruments and counting swabs.

'Very pretty little case, this, Sister. I like a tricky one to start the day, while I'm fresh. Puts me on my mettle, hmm? Let me have a couple of Allis forceps, my dear. Thank you—yes. Very pretty little case indeed. See, Jackson? That's a very cedematous loop indeed, isn't it? Yes. No wonder poor chap is in such a state. Everything all right at your end, Elliot? He's a bit blue down here.'

'Pretty good, sir,' Barney said. 'Hope he's relaxed enough?'

'A shade on the boardlike side, m'boy. Can you remedy that for me? Maybe I'm not as strong as I was, but it's certainly harder work to move these muscles than it was when I was a younger man. Eh, Sister?'

'Oh, sir, you're not *old*,' Sister Osgood said, and snickered, and Sir James peered at her over the top of his mask, and snorted cheerfully.

'Well, I don't know—don't know. I'm nearly at the third stage of a surgeon's career, you know! Just pull that retractor a little to the left, Jackson—yes, fine. Fine. A piece of catgut, Sister, and then I'll be ready for the diathermy. Yes, the third stage. Do you know the three stages of a surgeon's career, Sister?'

He took the piece of catgut from her hand and tied a suture with a deft twist of his wrists in their smooth golden brown gloves.

'No, sir,' Sister said, looking up at him with an appearance of breathless interest.

21

'What are they?'

Barney almost laughed aloud. The old bag! She'd heard this hoary old joke as often as the rest of them—Sir James told it at almost every operating session.

Sir James worked in silence for a moment, and then stretched his shoulders a little and turned his head so that Nurse Cooper could swab the beads of sweat from it.

'I'll tell you. The first stage is to get on.'

He paused, and taking a needleholder from Sister, began to put a running suture into the sheet of muscle under his fingers.

'The second stage is to get honour.' And he held out his hand for a pair of scissors which she slapped into it smartly.

'And the third stage is to get honest!' he finished triumphantly, looking round at all of them, and they laughed obediently. Sir James's jokes were so familiar now that Barney could have repeated them with him, word for word, pause for pause.

'Hey!' Sir James said suddenly. 'Who's that in the anaesthetic room? I won't have outside people hangin' around these theatres while I'm working, do you hear me, Sister? Told you that before—send him away!'

Barney turned his head to look through the glass panels of the theatre door, following Sir James's irritated glare. He could see the anaesthetic room quite clearly, and grinned a little. John Hickson.

22

He was leaning against the wall of the anaesthetic room where the drug tray was set, an expression of almost imbecilic hopefulness on his face as Nurse Cooper, in response to a jerk of the head from Sister Osgood, hurried through the swing doors to speak to him.

Poor Hickson, mesmerised by the pale blonde good looks of Nurse Cooper, produced a series of highly transparent excuses to spend time in the Private Wing theatres. Irritating little devil though he was, Barney couldn't help feeling sorry for him.

Nurse Cooper came back after a moment, her face pink and her eyes demurely cast down.

'Dr Hickson, sir,' she reported. 'He says please could he come and watch since he has a free period until the ward rounds at eleven and he'd very much like to learn from you.'

'No!' Sir James roared. 'He can do nothing of the sort! If the bad mannered young puppy hasn't the courtesy to come at the beginning of a list the way I did when I was a houseman he can go and whistle. Tell him to go away!'

And Nurse Cooper scuttled away, but didn't return for at least five minutes. After all, she had to see Dr Hickson out of theatre, didn't she? Only courtesy—

Sharply, Barney's amusement at this little byplay evaporated. The bag on the anaesthetic machine began to expand and collapse less vigorously, and with an uneven rhythm, and he put down the syringe with which he had just

23

given an injection of muscle relaxant, and slipped one hand under the sheet covering the patient's face to check the pulse at the temple. It was thin, and uneven, and Barney frowned.

At the site of the operation, Sir James was touching forceps with the diathermy point, and instruments clattered into the bowl Sister held out for him as each bleeding point was sealed with a faint hiss and a familiar acrid odour.

'Sir James!' Barney said sharply after a moment, and the surgeon turned his head.

'What's the matter, m'boy? He's nicely relaxed now, so not to fret—'

Barney shook his head worriedly. 'I don't understand this. His pulse is failing—'

'What? Sister, a hot swab—' Swiftly, Sister Osgood twisted a big abdominal swab in hot saline and gave it to Sir James, who covered the incision with it before turning his full attention to Barney.

'Now, what's his blood pressure?'

Barney was already checking it, and turned to Sir James with a puzzled look on his face. 'It's falling rapidly—I don't understand this— look, can you hold on while I give him some intravenous coramine?'

'Of course—' And Sir James folded his hands against the front of his gown and moved up the table to stand beside Barney and watch him closely.

Cooper had come back into theatre now, and at a signal from Barney, wheeled a small

24

trolley to his side and began to draw up a syringe of heart stimulant while he pulled back the covering sheet and exposed the man's arm. Then, he checked the pulse again, and felt himself whiten.

'Damn and blast—damn, damn, damn—the pulse has stopped—put a cardiac needle on— I'll inject straight into the heart—'

The silence in the theatre was so thick that it was like a tangible thing, only the faint hiss of the anaesthetic machine cutting into it. Barney moved with a swiftness he wouldn't have thought possible, ripping the gown back from the broad chest, now ominously still, and running his fingers over the ribs, seeking the rib space directly above the heart.

'Colin—take the respiration bag and keep pumping—keep his lungs ventilated—' and Jackson obediently took the bag in his gloved hand and began a rhythmic squeezing and relaxing that filled the lungs with air. The chest began to move again under the artificial respiration and Barney, taking a deep breath, slid the wickedly long needle on the syringe into the intercostal space above the heart.

As he withdrew the needle, and put one hand back on the pulse his face cleared for a moment as he felt the lurch that meant the heart had started to pump again. But the movements fluttered wildly, and then stopped again, and Barney looked up at Sir James almost piteously, and shook his head.

'I'll try direct massage,' the older man said crisply, and held out his hand to Sister Osgood.

She thrust a scalpel into it, and they watched breathlessly as the skin moved under Sir James's confident fingers. Barney, his fingers glued to the pulse at the temple, found himself praying, almost willing the heart to beat again, willing the pulse that was so ominously still to start its heavy throbbing.

It seemed to him that time stood quite still as Sir James worked, cutting swiftly through tissue to reach the silent heart, finding it, smoothly flexing his long spatulate fingers in an attempt to pump life and movement back into it.

And even when Sir James straightened up, and shook his head, and stood with his hands dangling helplessly at his sides, Barney still stood stupidly, feeling for a pulse beat that wasn't there, waiting for a still heart to start beating again.

'You might as well turn off the machine, Elliot,' Sir James's harsh voice cut through the silence, making Barney jump slightly.

'What?' he said stupidly.

'Turn off the machine,' Sir James said again, and then spoke more gently. 'Bad luck, m'boy. The man's dead.'

'But he can't be!' Barney said, staring at the older man and then down at the figure on the theatre table. 'He can't be—'

'I can assure you he is,' Sir James said dryly.

26

'Diagnosis may not be as strong a point with me as it is with some of the physicians, but I can assure you this man is dead.'

Barney swallowed, a suddenly dry throat making him feel sick, and he sat down heavily on the swivel chair at the head of the table, and automatically reached for the machine and turned the knob on the oxygen cylinder to the off position.

'I don't understand it,' he said dully. 'I don't understand it.' And then he looked up at Sir James and spoke with an almost pleading note in his voice. 'Sir James? He didn't bleed, did he—did he? Haemorrhage? Shock?'

Sir James began to peel off his gloves and shook his head, avoiding Barney's eyes.

'No,' he said gruffly. 'This isn't any surgeon's error, m'boy. It's yours, and only yours. The man died under anaesthetic.'

He looked up then, and said almost hopefully, 'Allergy? Unexpected allergic response to the anaesthetic?'

But Barney had to shake his head. 'No. I'd recognise that a mile off. This was— extraordinary. He was fine—fine. I examined him briefly in the anaesthetic room before I started because he was an emergency admission in the middle of the night and I hadn't had a chance to get to him earlier, but I had no doubts, none at all. He was in fine condition for an anaesthetic—an abdominal emergency admittedly, but a healthy man otherwise. I don't *understand* it—'

'Well, perhaps the inquest will tell us the answer. We'll see what the post mortem report suggests—' Sir James said, and Barney closed his eyes suddenly in sick apprehension.

'Inquest—post mortem—' he said, and then looked at Jackson almost appealingly. 'Colin? Will—you be involved? Or just me and Sir James?'

'I'll probably be called as a witness,' Jackson said in a flat voice. He had been standing staring down at the dead man on the table, showing nothing of what he felt in his face.

'I'm sorry for you, Elliot, but you'll have to face it. An inquest is obviously inevitable, and there's no way of knowing what the verdict will be. I'll do my best for you—I imagine Sir James will too—' Sir James nodded heavily. '—and as far as I can see there's been no negligence.'

'My God—if they say there was I could be struck off!' Barney said, his voice rising, and Jackson nodded, and looked at him very directly.

'Precisely, Elliot. But we'll do our best for you. And perhaps the post mortem will reveal a cause. In the meantime—I'm sorry, but I imagine Sir James will agree that we'd better get Steven Cantrell to do the rest of the list this morning. It—will give you a chance to recover. You've had a shock—'

He turned to Sir James, and raised his eyebrows. 'Are you prepared to go on in this
28

theatre, sir? Because the rest of this morning's patients *have* been prepared—'

'We'll use the second theatre, sir,' Sister Osgood said, all brisk efficiency. 'Nurse Cooper! Send for Gellard, and tell him to arrange to move this patient to the mortuary. And then come at once and help me prepare the other theatre. Hurry, girl—'

Sir James touched Barney's shoulder briefly, and then went out, dropping his gloves and mask and gown into the bucket by the door as he went, and Jackson followed him.

And Barney sat still in his swivel chair, beside the body of the man who had died under the anaesthetic he had given him, too stunned by what had happened to think clearly at all. All that seemed to stick in his mind was that a patient was dead, and he, Barney, would appear to be the cause of that death.

CHAPTER THREE

'Sitting there like a zombie isn't going to help much,' Lucy said with a display of calm practicality she wasn't really feeling. 'Have some coffee, and then *talk* about it. Here—' and she thrust the cup under his nose.

He'd come into Female Medical with a look of blind misery on his face that she could see even from half way down the long ward, where

29

she had been preparing the equipment for Mrs Chester's pylogram. He'd stood very still, just inside the double doors, his head held up in a defensive sort of way, and she had felt the familiar lurch deep inside that she always felt when she saw his square body and ugly kind face.

And then she had become aware of the wave of misery that was coming from him, and had said crisply to her Staff Nurse, '—here, Crowther—you finish this. I'll be back in a moment—' and had walked swiftly down the ward between the serried ranks of beds, and taken his elbow and steered him into her office.

He'd let her push him into a chair, let her put a cigarette between his lips and light it, saying nothing. And when she'd said gently, 'What's happened, Dr Elliot?' he'd lifted bleak grey eyes to her brown ones and said huskily, 'I've had a death. On the table.'

And that was all. He sat there, the cigarette sending faint tendrils of grey smoke through his lax fingers, staring into space, and she sat perched on the desk in front of him, her hands on her lap, looking at him with all the sympathy she was feeling on her expressive round face, wanting to take him in her arms and rock him back to happiness again.

But you couldn't do that to a member of the medical staff, however much you ached to do it, not when the only time you'd ever been that close to him was when he'd danced with you at a hospital ball. So she did the practical thing, and rang her bell for coffee, and when the orderly brought it, staring with a positively macabre curiosity at the silent man slumped in his chair, had sent her sharply away before pouring out a strong cupful.

'Talk about it, Dr Elliot,' she said again, gently, and then with a tentative movement, touched his hand.

He started, and looked up, and managed a twisted travesty of a smile that made her want to cry suddenly. It was absurd the effect this man could have on her.

'I'm sorry, Sister,' he said, and his voice was thick. 'I've had a—a shock.'

'Yes,' she said gently. 'I can see you have. Please, drink this. It will help—and then you can tell me about it—'

Obediently, he drank the coffee, and she watched him, and when he put the cup down said approvingly, 'That's better. You've got your colour back.'

'I feel better,' he said, and then tried to smile again. 'I'm sorry. I can't think why—I don't even know how I got here. Isn't that crazy? I just came here without knowing I was doing it.'

He put out a hand, and touched hers. 'You're good for me. I must have realised that and come for help. Thank you.'

Through the anxiety she felt for him an absurd little shiver filled her with pleasure, but she tried to ignore it.

'I'm glad you did. Now, what happened? You really must try to talk about it, you know. It must have been something pretty grim to have this effect on you. You aren't usually so—so easily bowled over.'

His hand was shaking slightly as he lit another cigarette, and he leaned back in his chair and looked at her apologetically.

'I'm sorry to behave so stupidly—like a junior nurse at her first operation or something. But I've never had a death on the table before, and this—this was so unexpected. He was fine, you see, absolutely fine! I gave him a very brief examination in the anaesthetic room—I mean, damn it all, it was an emergency, and Foster had seen him in the small hours. Anyway I gave him a perfectly straightforward anaesthetic and he—he just collapsed and died,' he finished lamely.

It took ten minutes of patient probing on Lucy's part to get the story out of him properly, but he managed to explain, and then started to shake again as he let shock and anxiety mount in him again.

'There'll have to be an inquest and a post mortem—and if they find I've—I was negligent in some way, I'll be struck off—don't you see? It's taken me almost ten years to get to this stage, and I was going to apply for a junior consultancy at Christmas, and then—and then—oh, *hell!*' and he put both arms on the desk before him and dropped his head to pillow it miserably.

'Oh, my dear, don't!' Lucy said softly and slipped from the desk to crouch beside his chair. 'Oh, please, don't upset yourself so! I'm sure you're panicking for nothing! I know it's an awful thing to have happened, but patients have died under anaesthetics before and no one was struck off for it! Aren't you exaggerating the whole thing, because it shocked you so?'

He raised his face, and it was blotched and heavy.

'No, I'm not exaggerating. You see, I—I should have examined him more thoroughly— shouldn't have assumed that Foster's examination was enough. I—the post mortem'll probably show some defect I should have recognised in advance. That's what I'm afraid of. And I—what would I do if I couldn't practice any more? What would I do?'

'Now, stop it!' and she made her voice sound sharp, though every bit of her wanted to soothe him, to cradle him in her arms and soothe him. 'You're just panicking. This was just one of those tragedies that happens sometimes and you aren't going to mend matters by behaving like this. For pity's sake, don't you realise that if you go around the place looking like this, people'll think you *were* negligent, and knew it? You really must calm down.'

He looked at her for a moment and then straightened up.

'Yes. Of course. My God, I'm sorry. Of

course, you're right. I *am* in a stupid panic. It's just that—my job means a lot to me.'

'Of course it does,' Lucy said, and stood up, awkwardly smoothing her apron. She had been very close to him for those few seconds and now it was her turn to be aware of feeling rather shaky about the knees. 'And it can go on doing so, I'm sure. You'll see.'

He stood up and put out a hand to take one of hers in it. 'Yes. Of course. Look, I'm sorry to have thrown this at your head. I just didn't know what to do—and as I say, you always make me feel—good. Do you mind?'

She looked up at him, and then let her eyes slide away, feeling her face redden foolishly.

'No, I don't mind. I'm—glad, really. I mean—it's nice to be—be useful.' And then trying to be practical again, the brisk ward sister, said, 'Now what? Will you do that job for the X-ray department? Mrs Chester's pylogram?'

He looked panicky again for a moment, and she shook her head slightly at him and said firmly, 'Yes. You must. Work has to be done. Everything's ready, and I'll call the X-ray department and tell them. OK? They're bringing up a portable machine because she can't be shifted down to the department. Come on now.'

By the time the X-ray department people had packed up their equipment and departed, he was in a much better frame of mind. He'd felt the hateful shakiness come back into his fingers as he tried to slip the needle of his syringe into the twisted gnarled vein in the crook of old Mrs Chester's elbow, but Lucy held out a swab, letting her hand rest near his, and he felt better, was able to control the trembling. It had been difficult to force himself to put the anaesthetic mask on the elderly face, but he found Lucy Beaumont close behind him again, and again, felt obscurely that it would be all right. And it was.

It had been a very light anaesthetic, and the old lady came round almost as soon as he turned off the machine, to start swearing with a fluency that was very funny, coming from so lavender-and-lace looking a person. And in the flurry of settling her again, he finally regained his equilibrium.

By the time Lucy escorted him, with perfect control, to the ward door he was much happier. He was so much happier that Lucy almost didn't say what she wanted to, for fear of upsetting him again, but she felt it was necessary.

'Dr Elliot—' she said diffidently, as they stopped by the big double doors. 'There's just one thing—'

He looked down at her, and smiled. 'I'm usually called Barney. My misguided father named me Barnabas after the church where he was curate when I was born, but Barney makes a more tolerable sound. You're Lucy,

35

aren't you?'

She blushed absurdly, and nodded, and then went on in a rush. 'Look, I suspect I know how the official mind works here, better than you do. I've been on the staff here for eight years, ever since I started my training—'

'That makes you—about twenty-six?' He really was feeling a great deal better.

She laughed. 'Perfect mathematics. I was twenty-six last week. But look, let me explain—and please, don't take it the wrong way—'

He sobered immediately. 'What is it?'

'Mr Stroud—the hospital secretary—well, he's the sort that plays safe all the time. If one patient falls out of bed, he makes you put the entire wardful into cot sides. And, after this morning—well—' she stopped, confused.

'After this morning in the private theatres, he isn't going to feel very safe with me,' Barney said flatly.

'Well, yes,' Lucy said awkwardly. 'I don't mean that he'll rush around blaming you, or anything, just that, well, he'll probably suggest that you—you don't take the major lists for a while. It'll be as much to protect you as the hospital, truly it will, so you mustn't let yourself get into a state about it—'

'I'll bet it will,' Barney said bitterly, and then managed a smile as he looked down at her anxious face. 'Bless you. Being warned that Stroud may make life awkward will certainly help me cope. You really have been splendid this morning, haven't you? Look—tonight, when you get off duty, let me buy you a drink, hmm? It's the least I can do, after all the coffee I've had on this ward. And you're easy to talk to. Please?'

If she hadn't been so upset for him she'd have wanted to dance a little pirouette. But she just said meekly, 'I'd like that.'

'The Ship in Bottle, then? Will that do?'

She laughed. 'Where else? It's our local, isn't it? I've heard rumours they're going to extend the tannoy call system to the Saloon bar there. It's the one place you can be sure of finding a doctor when you need one. About nine? I'm not off duty until half past eight.'

'About nine. I'll be there, crying into my beer.' But he smiled again as her face fell, and the worried look returned to it. 'Not really. But I'll look forward to seeing you. And thanks again—'

He touched her shoulder briefly, and went, leaving Lucy feeling extraordinarily confused. The one thing she had yearned for for weeks now had been just this—a chance to get to know Barney Elliot better. But what a hateful way for it to happen! She knew quite well that his anxiety was perfectly justified; that in the case of any unexplained death under dubious circumstances—and what could be more dubious than a death on the table, of an apparently healthy man?—officialdom bayed

37

for a scapegoat. And Barney seemed to be ideally suited at the moment for casting in the role.

She spent the rest of the day in a thoroughly confused condition, even forgetting to order the week's supply of stock drugs and medicines from the Pharmacy—an omission which was to complicate the ward's running not a little.

Lucy had been absolutely accurate in her forecast of official reaction to the morning's episode. Mr Stroud sent for Barney just before lunch, and a painful interview, during which Barney was hard put to it not to lose his temper, so sleekly did the hospital secretary put his point of view, sent his temporarily raised spirits plunging again. As he made his way to the doctors' quarters after assuring Mr Stroud with some bitterness that he would not work single handed, always using the help of his opposite number Dr Steven Cantrell, until after the inquest, even the thought of his appointment with Lucy Beaumont failed to make him feel anything but thoroughly miserable.

He had no appetite for lunch, so he bypassed the dining room, deciding to settle for a ham sandwich and coffee in the common room. He was standing by the table near the door, pouring his coffee, when Jeff Heath came in and slammed the door behind him.

Barney looked up in surprise. Jeff was one of the easiest going men on the staff, and it wasn't like him to display temper.

'What's up, Jeff? You look fit to hang someone.'

'Leave me alone, will you?' the other man said gruffly and hooked the bunch of path lab keys on to the board by the door, alongside several other sets. 'I've had about as much as I can take this morning. First three bloody technicians are off sick, so I'm running the damned laboratory single handed—well, the haematology lab, anyway—and now this!'

Behind him, the door swung again, and Colin Jackson came in, with John Hickson bustling behind. They too came to pour coffee, and Colin raised his head sharply when Jeff went on. 'The way Sir James went on, you'd think I'd just slopped any blood into the man, and not bothered to cross match—'

'Sir James? What about him?'

Jeff threw himself into one of the shabby armchairs and took the cup of coffee Barney brought him. Barney sat down too, and John Hickson came and joined them in their corner by the big window. Jeff drank some coffee, a little noisily, and then leaned over and took one of Barney's sandwiches before answering, with his mouth full.

'He's rampaging about like a bloody lunatic,' he said bitterly. 'To listen to him, you'd think he was the only surgeon operating here—not to mention the physicians. I've got a pile of work as high as a house to get through, and he sends me to vet a transfusion in the wing in the middle of the morning, and hang everyone else's urgent stuff! Not that he hadn't a fair enough reason, I suppose—'

He rubbed his face wearily, looking very young with his baby blue eyes and fair hair over a rubicund complexion.

Colin Jackson came over to him, and sat on the arm of his chair.

'What happened? Sir James left me to finish his list after doing the gastrectomy, and I've only just left theatre—'

'It's the gastrectomy that's the problem,' Jeff said. 'One hell of a problem. I tell you, this morning's been a right—'

'What *happened*?' Jackson said again, sharply. 'The operation went all right—he was fine when he left theatre—'

'With a blood transfusion going—I know,' Jeff said.

'He was anaemic on admission,' Colin said. 'That's why I asked for blood for him. Sir James agreed—it was a routine sort of thing. Nothing to worry about. I'd have given him the blood in advance if I'd had the chance, but the feller wouldn't come in in time. So we put it up in theatre. And he was fine when he went back to the ward. Sir James said he'd go and see him before he left—he had to go early to see a patient in Harley Street. One of his influential civil servants sent for him in the middle of the case—'

40

Jeff nodded heavily. 'I know all that. He told me, at some length, that my crass stupidity was mucking up his entire morning, quite apart from what it was doing to Quayle—'

'Oh, for heaven's sake, Jeff! Will you tell me what happened, or have I got to go over to the wing and find out for myself?' Colin snapped.

'He suddenly showed a reaction,' Jeff said heavily. 'Looked for all the world like the reaction you get when a patient gets an incompatible batch of blood. I told the old boy it couldn't be that, not possibly, but he just swore at me and told me to get the hell out, so I did.' He sounded very aggrieved. 'Honestly, these high powered consultants—they've got the manners of pigs. If I dared to speak to the most junior nurse the way that man spoke to me this morning there'd be all hell to pay—but he can get away with it! Sister was in the room, and young Caspar, and a junior nurse, and he swore at me as though I were a—a hospital porter or something. It just isn't good enough! Quite apart from implying I hadn't done my job properly and sent over incompatible blood for a patient!'

The door swung again, and Harry Caspar, the junior housesurgeon who alternated between the genito-urinary surgeons and Sir James's general surgery, came in, his face bleak and worried. When he saw Jeff, he turned as though to go out again, but Jeff jumped up, and shot across the room to grasp his elbow.

41

'Well?' he asked sharply. 'What's going on over there? Has he thrown you out, too?'

Harry reddened, and looked at the taller man with troubled eyes. 'Look, I'm sorry, Jeff. The old man'll be over in a minute and tell you himself, and I'd really rather not—'

'What do you mean, he's coming over? Hasn't he gone to Harley Street *yet*?' Peter asked.

Harry shook his head. 'Hardly. There's no end of a flap going on—'

Jeff almost shook him in frustration. 'What sort of flap? And why?'

'Quayle. He's dead,' Harry said baldly, and the room slid into immediate silence as the other men stared at him.

'Dead?' Colin was the first to speak, and he sounded stupefied. 'Dead? But why? He was in perfect shape when he left theatre!'

Harry looked acutely embarrassed, and moved away from Jeff to stand fiddling with the coffee things on the table by the door.

'Incompatible blood,' he said after a long pause, and then shrank as Jeff grabbed him by the shoulder and whirled him round.

'Incompatible blood? What the hell are you talking about! Just because that goddamned old bastard implied it, it doesn't give you licence to spread a slander like that!' he roared. 'Just you dare say a thing like that again, and I'll—'

'But it's true, Jeff—I'm sorry, but it's true—'

42

Harry Caspar cried, and then dodged as the other man tried to hit him.

There was a moment's flurry, as Colin Jackson grabbed Jeff, and Barney and John Hickson pulled Harry out of the enraged Jeff's reach.

It was Peter who brought some semblance of calm back into the room. He pushed Jeff into a chair, and stood in front of him as he spoke very sharply to Harry.

'Explain yourself,' he ordered briefly, and Harry, flexing his shoulders to get out of Barney's and John's grasp said sulkily, 'It's true. Sir James took a specimen of Quayle's blood and crossmatched it with the bottle he was having, and it showed clumping. The blood was incompatible, and that's all there was to it. And then the patient suddenly went into collapse and died. And that's all I know.'

Jeff sat very still in his chair, an expression of almost ludicrous horror on his face. And then Barney started to laugh, heard his own cracked unnatural laughter as though it came from someone else a long way away.

'Oh, my God, Jeff!' he gasped. 'Oh, my God! That makes two of us! Any more for the Killer's Stakes? Who'll be the next to dispose of a poor unsuspecting patient? Come on, you sick and lame and halt, come and get killed!'

And his laughter rose to an almost shrill pitch as the other men stood and stared at him in frozen horror.

CHAPTER FOUR

By teatime the entire hospital was buzzing with it. Ward maids stood in clusters in the corridors, their heads together as they surmised and gasped and tut-tutted agreeably; nurses made excuses to run errands to the Pharmacy or the laboratories just so that they could stop on the way and gossip about the news with other nurses similarly escaped from ward routine; even the patients sat around in wheelchairs in the ward day rooms and wondered and worried about it.

At top level the talk could not be described as mere gossip, but as Conference. Mr Stroud sat heavily in his swivel executive-type chair, with Sir James in the only other comfortable chair the room possessed. The others stood about awkwardly, their faces showing clearly just how they felt about the matter.

Jeff Heath and Barney were perched side by side on the deep window sill, Barney looking numbed, but a little less hopelessly miserable than he had. There was a sort of comfort in not being alone in his dilemma, a thought that made him feel faintly guilty as he looked at Jeff. Jeff just glowered heavily, but the sulkiness of his expression barely hid the real fear that underlay his anger.

On the other side of the room, the nursing

44

staff stood tidily together, Sister Osgood and Sister Palmer, from the second floor of the Private Wing, in uniform, and Staff Nurse Cooper in defiant mufti. It was her half day, after all, and worrying—and fascinating—though the situation was, she was justifiably annoyed at the interference with her free time.

Leaning against the wall beyond them, Harry Caspar, Derek Foster and Colin Jackson had schooled their faces into a polite blankness, though there was some sympathy to be seen in Harry's expression as he looked at the two men in the window seat from time to time.

There had been a moment's silence, and then Mr Stroud spoke again.

'I'm not quite sure what we can *do*, Sir James,' and there was a faintly pleading note in his voice. 'Not until the inquests show there is something to *be* done. It is quite possible, isn't it, that the post mortems on these—er—unfortunate patients will show understandable causes for their deaths? If we go off half cocked now, and start a great hue and cry all we'll do is disturb the hospital for no good reason, upset patients, and collect a lot of very unfortunate publicity. And I'm sure we all feel that it would be *most* undesirable to have the Royal dragged through the newspapers—'

'Look, Stroud,' Sir James growled, 'I'm as aware as you are of the undesirability of publicity. But I am also aware, as you apparently are not, that something is very amiss in this hospital—and as a senior consultant on the staff, bringing my private patients here, you must surely see that I have to be certain just what it is.' He paused significantly and then went on, 'Unless I can find out exactly what caused these deaths, I cannot possibly bring my private work here any more. If that is the price you are prepared to pay for keeping this matter under wraps, well and good—'

Mr Stroud immediately became very fussed. The revenue the Private Wing earned from Sir James's very rich private patients was essential to the hospital, despite the fact that it had far more National Health beds than private ones. And what was more, if Sir James stopped working in the wing, it was odds on several of the other consultants would follow suit. A possibility like that was almost worse than a nine days newspaper wonder about patients dying under odd circumstances.

On the other hand, such publicity in itself would have the effect of frightening potential private patients away. Stroud was firmly pinned in a cleft stick, and the way he fiddled with papers on his desk, and ummed and erred showed how helpless he felt, faced with the implacable Sir James.

'But what can I do?' he said again, and looked round at the other people in the room, who stared silently back at him. 'I've called everyone who might possibly know anything to this conference, as you asked, Sir James, but for what purpose, I—'

'To see if we can discover something from talking about what happened,' Sir James said, and turned heavily in his chair to look at the eight people ranged around him. 'Let's start with the strangulated hernia. Who saw him first?'

'Night Sister,' Derek Foster said promptly. 'He came in by ambulance from the docks, and Sister saw him in Casualty, reckoned he was an acute abdomen of some kind, and got the man who'd come with him from his ship to sign a consent form for an operation, just in case. I found out that much when they called me to see the bloke around five o'clock this morning.'

'Has his ship been notified of his death?' Sir James asked.

'No,' Stroud cut in. 'It sailed this morning at six. The Polish Embassy are listed as the next of kin, in this case. They've been notified—and I'm relieved to be able to say they don't seem particularly bothered. I got the impression, talking to them this morning, that they almost expected him to succumb to his operation,' and he couldn't resist shooting a malicious glance at Sir James's oblivious back.

'So at least we've no irate relatives to contend with,' Sir James said. 'Only an extremely irate surgeon—me.'

He turned then to Barney, who jumped a

47

little. 'Now, Elliot. I want a blow by blow account of that anaesthetic. At the time it happened I was disturbed enough—but in the light of this latest development, I am even more disturbed—and convinced that there was something extremely odd about this death. And I want to know what you did, and what you think.'

'I can tell you what I did, sir,' Barney said helplessly. 'But no more than that. I mean, I was knocked sideways by it—still feel extraordinarily bothered. But *why* it happened—I wish to God I knew! As far as I'm concerned the sooner it can be sorted out the better I'll be pleased. If there's been some dirty work going on, I want it uncovered, because as things stand now, I'm right in line for being struck off at worst—and being set right back in my chosen speciality at the very least. So if anyone thinks there's the remote chance of there being a case for the police here, I want to see 'em called in. And to hell with the publicity,' and he glared defiantly at Stroud.

'No doubt,' Sir James said dryly. '*If* some outside agent played a part in the death. But before we can be sure of that—and I'm damned if I'm just going to assume it—I want to be sure that there hasn't been some old fashioned common or garden bloody inefficiency here! And I warn you fairly, young man, that if there has I personally will do all in my power to have it dealt with very severely. If there's one thing I

48

won't tolerate in any shape or form it's inefficiency—and the only thing I abominate more is attempts to cover it up! That's why you're all here—to corroborate what everyone else has to say, and show us immediately if there has been some negligence. So, I want a clear account of what you did this morning!'

Barney flushed a heavy brick red, and there was a faint rustle of movement around the room. But Sir James ignored it, just fixing Barney with his glare.

'Right!' Barney said, keeping his voice as even as he could. 'Since we're working along the lines that a man is guilty until proven innocent—'

'Now, we'll have none of that!' Sir James barked. 'This isn't a court of law, and nothing that's said here will ever get to a court of law if I have my way. But I want this business thrashed out, and thrashed out it will be! So start talking!'

How he managed it he'd never know. He spoke in a level even voice that belied the sick fear that filled him, and the overlay of deep anger at Sir James's autocratic ways. He told the silent listening room of everything that had happened, of his conversation with Nurse Cooper, even about the ridiculous little bit of fussing over the unlocked anaesthetic room door (at which Nurse Cooper flushed a sick red and then went pale, and Sister Osgood shot a malevolent look at her). He described the

49

anaesthetic he had given, punctiliously announcing the dosages as well as the drugs he had used, the way he had double checked the anaesthetic machine after Gellard had checked it—pointing out with some satisfaction that this was his normal practice—and going on until the point was reached at which the patient's heart had begun to fail. His voice faltered a little then, but he went on as carefully as he could.

'The man seemed quite well until that point—normal good deep respirations, even blood pressure. And then his breathing became very shallow, and he looked very pale. He started to sweat too, and I wondered if he was beginning to come out of deep anaesthetic to a shallower level—I'd kept it fairly light deliberately because he was in a state of shock on admission. But it wasn't that—and then—then—'

It was difficult to describe the way he had tried to resuscitate the man, the giving of the heart stimulants, the cardiac massage, but doggedly he went on.

'—and then you said he was dead, and I—I couldn't believe it. And that's all I know,' he finished.

There was a moment's silence, and then Sir James nodded in a satisfied way.

'Right. I can certainly corroborate what happened once the man came into theatre. So can you, Jackson.'

Colin nodded wordlessly.

'You left out the fact that that impertinent young houseman came sniffing around— what's his name?'

'What? Oh, John Hickson,' Barney said. 'I didn't think that was significant.'

'Everything is significant,' Sir James snapped. 'Now, Staff Nurse—what's your name? Cooper? Can you corroborate what Dr Elliot has told us? About what happened before I arrived?'

Nurse Cooper gulped, and whispered, 'Yes sir.'

'Speak up, girl! In every detail?'

She nodded. And then jumped as Sister Osgood spoke very sharply.

'This matter of the unlocked anaesthetic room—' she said, and her voice was harsh as she looked at Cooper. 'Why was it locked in the first place? I don't normally expect the anaesthetic room to be locked overnight. The anaesthetic machines are locked into the main store room, and the theatre unit as a whole is locked up—so why? *I* find that odd enough to be worth discussing,' and she turned and looked at Sir James in a challenging way.

Nurse Cooper looked miserably at Sister Osgood, and swallowed again, very near to tears.

'I—I'm sorry, Sister,' she said.

'What is all this?' Sir James said quickly. 'Something odd about an unlocked door?

51

Explain yourself, girl.'

Nurse Cooper was now frankly crying, and found it difficult to speak, but when Sister Osgood said bitingly, 'Explain at once, Nurse,' she gulped, and began to speak.

'Sir James's list starts very early,' she said in a husky voice. 'And it's always such a rush and panic to get set up in time for him—and Sister gets—gets angry if everything isn't just perfect when she comes on duty just before the list starts. So—so—well, I try to save time, you see. And—and the night before Sir James is operating, I set up the anaesthetic room, and lock the door, ever so carefully, so that I can just get on with setting up the actual theatre in the morning. Only this morning it was unlocked, and I *know* I locked it last night—'

'You do *what?*' Sister Osgood sounded as horrified as she would have done had Nurse Cooper confessed to throwing orgiastic parties in the operating theatres. 'You do *what!?*'

Nurse Cooper turned on her, goaded to indiscretion. 'Well, I do—I always have. I can't help it! You make such a hullabaloo if everything isn't spot on, and there just isn't time! So I put out the gowns, and set up the agony wagon—I mean, the patient's trolley, and set in the anaesthetic machine after Gellard's checked it, and put out the drugs, and everything! And if I had another junior on with me in the morning, I wouldn't have to!' And she burst into noisy tears, turning her

52

back on Sister Osgood's scandalised face.

'Stop that caterwauling at once,' Sir James roared. 'Now we're beginning to get somewhere! You say the anaesthetic machine was *not* locked up safely last night? That it could have been tampered with? Is that the explanation of this wretched sailor's unfortunate death?' He turned on Barney then.

'Are you sure that machine was fit to use? Was the oxygen coupled up properly? You didn't give the man carbon dioxide instead of oxygen, did you?'

'No,' Barney said dryly. 'I read that novel too—and there was nothing like that. I know an oxygen deficiency when I see one—and I tell you I checked the machine myself—'

Colin Jackson's voice rose sharply above the sound of Nurse Cooper's gulping sobs. 'It can't be that, sir,' he said.

'Why not?'

'Because Cantrell used it for the second patient—Quayle. When he came to take over from Elliot, the other machine had been borrowed by private maternity for an urgent high forceps delivery—so he used the machine Elliot had used, without any trouble. Quayle didn't die under *his* anaesthetic.'

'Hmm.' Sir James sat and brooded for a moment. 'Of course. You're quite right. He didn't. And that brings us to this second fiasco. Quayle. There was nothing wrong with that man but a gastric ulcer and a little anaemia.

Now, what happened to him? We'll come back to the question of the anaesthetic room and what relevance it may have had to the sailor's death in a moment—'

'Just a minute, sir,' Colin Jackson said again. 'I think we can demolish the anaesthetic room idea right now. The theatres are locked overnight as a routine, aren't they?' He turned to Nurse Cooper, now mopping her blotched and swollen face with a scrap of handkerchief. 'Were the theatres locked this morning when you came on duty?'

'Yes sir.' She spoke eagerly. 'Oh, yes sir. I got the keys as usual from the porter's lodge in the main hall as I came on—they were locked all right.'

'So the fact that the anaesthetic room was unlocked doesn't signify anything,' Colin said crisply. 'I can only suppose that Nurse Cooper did *not* lock it last night as she assures us she did. She is mistaken, and forgot. Either way, the machine was safely out of reach of any unauthorised meddling—and as I've pointed out, Cantrell used it safely *after* the death.'

Nurse Cooper opened her mouth to argue, but at the sight of Sister Osgood's sharp glance subsided, and Sir James nodded.

'You have a point there. Now, Heath— about this man Quayle. I know the cause of his death, even before any damned post mortem proves it. He had an incompatible transfusion. Now, what have you got to say to *that*?' and he glared at the heavy sulky face of the man in the window seat.

'Nothing,' Jeff said, in as strong a voice as Sir James's own. 'All I know is that I got a specimen of blood yesterday from the Private Wing with a request for crossmatching of a pint of blood. I crossmatched two pints, one for a reserve, and put them in the haematology lab refrigerator. The blood was collected this morning by a ward nurse, and the transfusion set up in theatre—by Cantrell, I believe. I can swear to you the blood was Group A, the same as the specimen I was sent—a specimen labelled Quayle. Of course, if I was given the wrong sample, I can't be blamed—'

'You certainly received the right sample, Dr Heath,' Sister Palmer said in her soft lilting Welsh voice. 'I can guarantee that. I took the blood myself, because both Mr Jackson and Mr Caspar were busy yesterday when the patient came in, and I labelled it myself, and brought it over to the lab on my way off duty at teatime. I put it into your own hand, Dr Heath, as you'll perhaps remember.'

Jeff rubbed his face wearily. 'Yes I remember. Well, I don't understand it. I *know* I checked the right blood and labelled it properly before putting it in the fridge. I can't say more than that.'

'Jeff—could one of the technicians have meddled in some way?' Barney said gently. 'You aren't the only person who uses the lab, after all, pathology registrar though you are.'

Jeff shook his head heavily. 'No. I told you—they're all off sick with this damned gastro-enteritis infection that's been causing so much trouble. I even had to unlock the labs and set them up myself yesterday and today. There's only me.'

There was a silence again, as they all realised just how black things looked for Jeff—even blacker than for Barney, equivocal as Barney's position clearly was. Then Mr Stroud spoke again.

'So what has all this shown us, Sir James? That two patients have died who shouldn't have—and we all knew that. But we're no nearer to knowing *why* apart from a lot of conjecture about locked doors, and unlocked doors, and incompatible blood being given. Where do we go from here?'

Sir James stood up, and began to prowl heavily about the room.

'I'm damned if I know. I'm damned if I do. I thought we'd find out more—elucidate matters a little—and all we've done is cloud the question even more. I just don't understand it.'

He came and stood in front of Stroud, then, leaning on his desk on clenched fists.

'But I'll tell you this much, Stroud. I'm not satisfied, d'you hear me? Not satisfied. And if this matter isn't cleared up, and cleared up very soon, I'll raise such hell for you and for the staff of this hospital that'll shake you rigid. I'm not ruining my practice by letting people think my patients die like flies for no reason! You get the answer to this, and see to it that the people at fault are dealt with, or you'll have more trouble on your hands than you can imagine. Understand? Right. So you decide what to do. I agree with Elliot there—this is a police matter, I want to know *why* those men died, and how, and I want to know fast. So make up your mind to it—either you find out what happened here today, or I send the police in.'

And he turned on his heel and marched out of the room, leaving the people behind him in a stunned sick silence.

'Erhrrm! Yes. Well,' Stroud said eventually, and rearranged the papers on his desk again. And then jumped to his feet and began to prowl up and down the room, in an unconscious and rather funny parody of Sir James.

'What does he want me to do? I can't go calling in police, not without something tangible to tell them!'

'Aren't two dead bodies tangible enough for you?' Colin Jackson said, and turned on his heel, making for the door. 'I've got some work to do, if no one else has. But I'll tell you this much before I go, Mr Stroud. If you do call the police in, you needn't look to me to co-operate with them. No damned great bumbling policeman is going to set foot in any ward in which I have patients, understand? And no one

57

can make me let them in, because you know damned well that in such matters I'm in charge. *No one* goes near any surgical patient in this place without my consent and that's flat. Caspar, I'm going to do a round on Male Surgical. You'd better come too.'

Obediently, Harry followed him, shrugging his shoulders at Barney and Jeff in an attempt to indicate his sympathy. Stroud's voice pulled them both back.

'My God!' Stroud said explosively. 'My God! Haven't I got enough to put up with without a bunch of surgeons behaving like bloody prima donnas!' And then he saw the frozen look on Sister Osgood's face and coughed and turned to Barney and Jeff.

'Look, I'm sorry about all this, and sympathise with the way you must be feeling. And I daresay you *would* like the police in to sort it all out, and make things look—well, better for you. But you must see that my hands are tied. I can't report anything until I know what I'm reporting—and I won't know that till the post mortems are done. I hope they'll be done tomorrow some time—'

'Not here they won't be,' Jeff said in a surly voice.

'Why not?'

'Because I'm the pathologist here, remember? And I do the P.Ms. I hardly imagine I'd be allowed to do those, under the circumstances.'

58

The expression of dismay on Stroud's face was ludicrous.

'Oh, no! That means I'll have to get the pathologist from Queen's to come over—and the chances are we'll have to wait until he can fit in a visit here. Oh, damn, damn, damn—'

The door opened, and the rather scrawny middle aged woman who was Stroud's secretary came in, her eyes darting from face to face eagerly as she sought a scrap of gossip— any scrap—to spread among the rest of the hospital's clerical staff.

'What do you want?' Stroud snapped.

'It's Mr Bruce, sir. He wants to talk to you very urgently. Says it really is very important.'

'Bruce? Bruce?'

'Chief Pharmacist. You're in a bad way this afternoon, Mr Stroud!' Derek Foster said. 'You can't even remember the names of your own people!'

Stroud ignored him. 'Tell Mr Bruce I can't possibly see him now. I'm very disturbed— very—and late into the bargain. I should have been out of here half an hour ago—and I'm serving no good purpose by staying any later. Tell him to come over in the morning—half past nine.' And the secretary nodded and, unwillingly, went away.

He turned and looked at the people standing around him, and again a look of helplessness swept over his jowly face. 'I really must call this—er—conference to an end. I'll think about what to do in the morning. In the meantime, good afternoon.'

And Mr Stroud went over to the window and stood staring down at the ambulance-busy courtyard below as they filed silently out of the room.

CHAPTER FIVE

'You're being remarkably foolish,' Lucy told her mirrored reflection sternly, and then childishly stuck out her tongue, the way she had been used to when she was a child and feeling rather bothered. And then she dropped her hairbrush, and went and sat on her bed to stare unseeingly out of the window at the garden gleaming dully in the deep blue of an early summer night.

The window was open, and she could smell the heavy sweetness of late lilac and a few early roses, and the faint haze of newcut grass left by the efforts of the gardener that afternoon. He was a hardworking gardener, who had created a small gem of greenery and shrubbery and flowers from an unpromising patch of sooty London earth tucked away behind the hospital, within spitting distance of the oily noisy smelling docks. But Lucy was, for once, unappreciative of his efforts.

She could hear, from the main door of the

Nurses' Home a few yards away—for her room was on the ground floor, a privilege granted only to Sisters—the voices of the young students waiting for their dates, the giggles and silly inconsequential chatter of the young. And suddenly felt stirred up and miserable, yet happy too. It was an extraordinary mixture of sensations.

'You *are* being foolish,' she told herself again. 'Aren't you? It's because it's summer, and the short warm nights bring all your hormones out in a rush. That's all. You can't possibly be in love with the man—can you? Those silly girls, *they* go falling in love with housemen—' and a sudden burst of laughter from the students outside made her grimace wryly, 'but they're moppets of eighteen or so, while you, you're a grown woman of twenty-six. There's more than a quarter of a century behind you, yet you go and get wobbly kneed about a houseman, and an ugly houseman at that, for all the world like a first year lamb. Where's your pride? Where's your sense?'

But it made no difference. She still felt a surge of frightened elation when she thought of her meeting with Barney, the meeting for which she was right now supposed to be dressing.

But still she lingered. In an odd way it made her feel more adult, more in control of her emotions, not to rush through dressing and doing her face and hair. So she went over to the window, and perched on the sill, and looked out.

The smell of the garden filled her nostrils, made her breathe deeply with an intense sensuous pleasure, and she let her gaze wander, taking in the warm red brick of the walls of the private block beyond, the golden squares of uncurtained windows through which the tops of bed curtains could be seen, and the deep sighing shadows under the great copper beech that had somehow survived the years of growth in the unhealthy air of Dockland.

'The thing is,' the insistent little voice in her mind started again, 'the thing is, you're feeling bothered not because he asked you out for a drink, but because of the *reason* he did. If he'd asked you last week, even yesterday, you'd just have been pleased, and hopeful—admit it, hopeful—but not as you are now, with depression mixed up with the pleasure. It's because he asked you out of a sort of gratitude. Because you helped him cope with a crisis of his own.'

Irritably she kicked the wall beneath the sill, and ran her fingers through her short curly hair.

'Yes, but,' she argued back. 'He *did* come to you for help, didn't he? He might have gone anywhere in the hospital, gone to anyone else. He could have gone to see Avril Gold, up on Orthopaedics—she's such a glamour pants, everyone makes a bee line for her. And I don't

62

blame them.' She brooded for a while on Sister Gold's superior charms. 'But he *didn't*. He came to you. Doesn't that help?'

There was a movement in the garden, and more to still the silent argument in her head than because of genuine interest she leaned out to see who it was. There was a faint gleam of white moving along the path that ran from the Private Wing to the covered way that led to the Pharmacy and Path lab block, but she couldn't see who it was. Odd. Who could be going to those departments at this time of night? They'd been locked and deserted for hours now.

And then, above the distant rumble of the traffic in the main road beyond the hospital, she heard a faint chiming, heard the clock melodiously announce each quarter and then the hour, and jumped up, and in a sudden fever of activity brushed her hair again, and grabbed her coat, and ran from the room. Whatever the reason, whatever it meant, Barney had asked her to have a drink with him and she did want to, very much. And now she was late.

* * *

She stood inside the door of the saloon bar, blinking a little in the blaze of light, her hands thrust deep into the pockets of her camel hair jacket, her legs in their striped brown trousers spread wide, a little defiantly.

She always felt rather awkward, meeting

63

people in pubs. With her rather rigid Calvinistic upbringing—her mother had been a daughter of a Scots parson—pubs had for her a raffish air of wickedness that they would never lose.

Not that the 'Ship in Bottle' was an ordinary pub. Built with a wealth of gilt, plum-coloured paint, engraved glass, and glaring-bright lights in Victorian times to satisfy the thirsts of burly dockers, it had long ago become an extension of the hospital's staff common rooms, set as it was right opposite the hospital gates.

The landlord—and the present one had been in charge for the best part of thirty years, right through the flaming roaring horror of the blitz—was almost one of the hospital staff himself. He knew everyone, from the most junior porter to the most senior consultant, had known most of those senior consultants since their distant student days when they had been ribald beer-drinking rugby-playing Dressers walking the wards behind black coated medical men of the really old school.

At this moment he was hurrying past the door with a tray load of thick mustard be-daubed sandwiches and a pot of his own make of pickled onions, and he stopped and peered at Lucy as she stood hesitantly looking through the crowded bar for Barney.

'Well, now, it's—Nurse Beaumont, isn't it? Long time since you were in here, my dear. Let me see, you used to go about with that feller

64

that went into general practice over to the Isle of Dogs. Er—Piggot, wasn't that his name? Yes, Piggot. Best scrum-half the hospital rugger team ever 'ad—'

Lucy went pink at being reminded so unexpectedly of that old if rather torrid love affair that had fizzled out so suddenly when Victor Piggot had qualified and she had become a Staff Nurse—so long ago, now.

'Hello, Chalky,' she said. 'It has been a long time, I suppose. I hadn't realised how long. It's Sister Beaumont, now, you know. I got Female Medical a year ago.'

'Did you now!' the landlord said admiringly, and then mopped his shining bald head with one large hairy fist. 'Well, you deserve it—always was a smart girl, wasn't you? Look, I've got a bunch of starving medical students over there bawling for this nosh—so I'd better 'and it over before they wreck the place.'

His serene expansive grin made it very plain he did not really entertain any such fears, and indeed, there was no reason why he should. He was a huge man, six foot three and with the build of one of the great ships on the docks he had kept fed and supplied with liquor all these years.

'Who was you looking for, lovey?'

'Dr Elliot. Do you know him?'

'I knows 'em all, my dear. Over by the joanna—there 'e is. And I'm glad you're 'ere if it's you he's been waiting for. In a right

65

miserable mood he is, not a bit like himself. Not that I blame 'im, mind. Not after what happened over there today,' and he jerked his head in the general direction of the hospital.

'You know then?' Lucy said sharply.

He laughed as he moved away towards the group of noisy young men in the far corner of the crowded bar, who were now banging heavily on the tables with tankards.

'Bless yer, lovey, there's nothin' happens over there as I don't know about sooner or later—mostly sooner. They all come and tell Chalky White the news, they do. Go on, my dear—go and look after poor ol' Barney, before he ruins his beer with cryin' in it—'

She pushed through the crowds to the corner where the large and battered old upright piano held pride of place, its red silk linings behind the fretted fronts worn and stained with age.

The men standing about with pint tankards in their hands moved politely out of her way, and she smiled gratefully up at them. There had been a time, early in her training, when she had been afraid of these big rough-tongued men, but that was before a period of night duty on casualty had taught her how essentially gentle and courteous dockers could be.

Barney indeed looked miserable. He was sitting sideways on the old piano stool, a cigarette in one hand, the other counting the yellowing keys on the instrument, and she felt her heart twist with love and pity as she looked at him.

She stood still for a moment, in the shadow of a couple of men who were arguing with friendly acrimony about the rival merits of a pair of greyhounds, and looked at him as dispassionately as she could. Why did she find him so damnably attractive?

No one could call him good looking, with his rough hair in its vague sort of mouse colour. Sometimes, when he first came on duty, it looked tidy, brushed down with a wetted brush, but mostly it looked as it did now, a rather unkempt broomhead, standing up in rough spikes. And his face—square and heavy, with a deep lower lip below an absurdly narrow upper one. A curious mouth, both sensuous and ascetic at the same time, a mouth to make one shiver most agreeably when one looked at it.

And his body, as square and heavy as his face. He can't be more than about five foot eight or so, she thought, but that's fine with me, seeing I'm only five foot three. Maybe I like the squareness of him because I'm undoubtedly on the round side myself? Does he make me feel comfortable for that reason? But that can't be enough to make me fall head over ears as I have—

And then he looked up and saw her, and she knew that if there was one physical feature he had that could make her melt it was his eyes. Wide, heavily fringed with lashes much darker than his hair, tipped up at the corners, and with blue lights in their translucent grey depths. A baby who inherited those eyes would be a very beautiful baby, she thought—and blushed at the idea.

'Lucy,' he said, and smiled, and she smiled back, not caring whether or not her pleasure in seeing him showed all over her face.

'I'm sorry I'm late,' she said, and came and stood beside him. 'Feeling better? Or just plain lousy?'

'Just plain lousy. Or I was. It's nice seeing you. Have a drink.'

Lucy, brought up by the many impecunious medical students she had known to consider their shallow pockets, nodded and said simply 'Cider,' and he went away to the bar, to return a few minutes later with a half of mild and bitter for himself and her cider tinkling with ice in a tall glass. A Dockland pub it might be that Chalky ran, but he knew better than to serve cider any way other than well iced, on a warm June night.

They drank silently for a moment, and then Lucy said, 'You shouldn't feel quite as bad as you did. Not since this afternoon's business.'

'You've heard?'

She raised expressive eyebrows. 'Of course! Sister Palmer told the world at supper tonight. The place is sizzling with it. But at least it means you and Jeff Heath are in the same boat now.'

68

He looked up at her. 'Perspicacious girl! The same thought had occurred to me, and then I felt a right bastard, because Jeff's in a much worse mess than I am. I mean, no one has accused me of making any mistakes as such—I'm just *suspected* of some sort of negligence. But Jeff—well, it looks as though he crossmatched the wrong blood, and who can prove he didn't?'

He brooded silently for a moment, and then spoke with conviction. 'I'll never believe Jeff did any such damnfool thing. Not Jeff. He's the most pernicketty careful sort of feller! If it had been John Hickson, now, I'd have believed it. For all his fussing he's a useless chap—makes more stupid errors than the whole staff put together. But Jeff? Never.'

He offered Lucy a cigarette from a battered pack, and she leaned forwards, hoping he wouldn't see the way her lips trembled as she held her face up to meet the flame of his lighter. But he just said, 'I like your perfume—' and smiled at her again.

There was a silence between them for a while, as they sat side by side on the old piano stool, staring at the people filling the bar. For Lucy, it was a silence filled with feeling, with an awareness of the warmth of his body beside her, an awareness of the return of that absurd desire to hold his weary head in her arms and soothe him.

And for Barney, it was a silence that was also

filled, with mixed inconsequential thoughts about this girl beside him. He looked at her, turning his head slightly, and he liked what he saw. Her round face with the high fresh complexion that even eight years in London hadn't taken from her, the dark curly hair, the pointed chin above the roll neck of the white cotton pullover she was wearing under the camel coat.

She became aware of his gaze, and turned and looked at him, and reddened in a way he thought delightful.

'Thank you for coming here tonight,' he said simply.

'Thank you for asking me, kind sir,' she said promptly, with an air of flippancy she wasn't feeling.

'I should have asked you out long ago, you know. I've wanted to.'

She bent her head to look with apparently absorbed interest at her hands, with their sensibly square cut nails and the faint redness her work gave them.

'Really? I—would have come then, too.'

'I was a bit scared of you.'

She stared at him then, and laughed. 'Scared? Of me? Oh, come on! No one's scared of me! Not even my most junior nurses! Why should you be?'

He looked a little sheepish. 'I don't know. Maybe because—oh, you looked so *nice*. Do look nice, I mean. Not like that Gold girl. I've taken *her* out, but then, who hasn't? You know where you are with Gold, but with you—well, I wouldn't have known, so I—I was nervous.'

'I think that's a compliment,' she said, a little breathlessly. 'Anyway, I'm going to treat it like one. So thank you.'

The silence that then descended on them could have been embarrassing, but just then Jeff Heath came pushing through the crowd towards them, and they both greeted him with a sort of relief.

'Jeff!' Barney jumped up, and dragged towards them a chair that another man was purposefully making for. 'Come and join us, and we can moan on each other's shoulders.'

Jeff glowered at the discomfited man whose chair had been taken from him, and sat down firmly, and the three of them sat and looked at each other.

'Hello, Lucy.' Jeff said. 'How's things?'

'Not so bad,' Lucy said, and grinned at him. She was quite fond of old Jeff, had always been so. He had originally trained at the Royal, so she had known him for years, unlike Barney, who had only come to his present job fairly recently, from Queen's, the hospital five miles away in a slightly more salubrious part of London.

'How's with you? Or is that a stupid question?'

'Bloody stupid,' Jeff said without rancour. 'Seeing I've been accused today of polishing off

71

one of Sir James's pet patients. Apart from that small thing, life couldn't be sweeter.'

'Well, we share the running for the top of the old so-and-so's hate stakes,' Barney said. 'I'm just as much in trouble as you are, and with less evidence.'

Jeff went a brick red, and opened his mouth, but Barney jumped in quickly.

'Christ! I didn't mean that—I'm in such a state, I don't know what I'm saying. I just mean that someone obviously meddled with the blood you crossmatched, while at the moment all that seems to be against me is vague suspicion—and I swear that's harder to bear.'

Jeff subsided, and looked consideringly at Barney for a moment before speaking.

'You really think someone meddled with the blood?'

'What else? If you say you crossmatched, you did. If the blood in the bottle wasn't Group A, and you said it was, then obviously someone meddled. It's clear as day—'

'But they don't believe me!' Jeff said. 'You heard that old bastard this afternoon! He obviously doesn't believe me!'

'Has anyone checked the label?' Lucy said practically.

They turned and looked at her.

'What did you say?' Jeff said after a moment.

'She said, "has anyone checked the label?"' Barney was staring at Lucy. 'Oh, my God. The most obvious thing in the world, and none of us thought of it. Has anyone checked the label?'

He turned back to Jeff, excitedly. 'Look, the label will carry the grouping, won't it? It always does.'

Jeff nodded.

'Right. There'll still be some blood left in the bottle, won't there? They're sent back to the haematology lab unwashed?'

Again Jeff nodded.

'So, if we check the blood that's left in the bottle with another bottle of known Group A blood, we'll be able to prove that somehow the contents were changed. And that you weren't at fault—that you *had* crossmatched the original contents properly—'

Jeff shook his head. 'It sounds logical, Barney, but it isn't. I mean, for God's sake, who in his right mind would go and change the blood in a bottle? Not that you can, anyway. Those bottles are well sealed, you know. Any tampering would stick out like the traditional sore thumb.'

'I don't know who, or why, or even how! I'm just saying it *could* have happened. If we can prove it did, by checking, then we can go and tell Stroud he's bloody well *got* to call in the police, no matter what he wants, and no matter what Colin Jackson says—'

'Colin Jackson!' Jeff said bitterly. 'I swear he thinks of nothing but *his* status, and *his*

73

importance, and *his* superiority to everyone else. The way he's behaving it's obvious he thinks we're both in cahoots with each other to kill off patients just to make life difficult for him. He makes me sick!'

'You talkin' about Colin Jackson?'

Jeff whirled and looked up as Chalky reached over to collect their empty glasses.

'He's a right moaner, he is. Always been the same, 'e 'as, long as I've known him. Can't help it though. Comes of goin' into medicine late in life. He was gone thirty, you know, when 'e started medical school. Must be—oh, well past forty-five by now. And never got no further than RSO, neither. Nor will he, bad tempered old devil. You gotta 'ave more than talent to get on in hospital, and well I know it.'

'Do you?' Lucy tried to sound interested, as the other two leaned back in their seats again, feeling somehow that it was necessary to behave as normally as possible. It wouldn't do, she felt obscurely, to let Chalky know too much about what happened over at the hospital, least of all that the three of them suspected that a deliberate attempt had been made to kill Quayle via his blood transfusion—an attempt that had succeeded. Dockers and hospital people weren't the only ones whose regular custom Chalky enjoyed. Plenty of Fleet Street men came down to the 'Ship in Bottle', and would soon winkle such a story out of the garrulous Chalky. And Lucy

74

shared with most hospital people a horror of newspaper publicity about their beloved Royal.

'Not 'arf!' Chalky said with relish. He leaned comfortably against the piano, obviously settling himself for a long session, and Lucy's heart sank. She felt, rather than saw, equal chagrin on Barney's part, but she smiled up at the big old man and said encouragingly, 'What do you mean?'

'Well, take the old basket himself—Sir James Custerson Weller,' and he rolled the syllables round his tongue as though they were edible. 'I've known him since he was common or garden Jimmy Weller. And he was no great shakes as a student, I'll tell you that for nothing. Just scraped his first MB, he did, and drove 'em mad with his daft ways when 'e was a dresser. Anyway, he's got that somethin' more. A sort of talent for people, you could call it. Don't matter how good you is at your job, if you haven't got this talent for people, you'll get nowhere. Like Colin Jackson won't, only don't tell 'im I said so. But Jimmy Weller—he's got it. He talked 'imself right to the top in no time, talked himself into his knight'ood— Custerson-Weller! 'N't it ridiculous? Talked himself out of trouble when that there woman died under the knife—'

Lucy looked up, sharply. She hadn't been paying much attention, letting her thoughts pleat themselves busily round the matter of the transfusion bottle. 'What was that?'

'The woman that died on the table!' Chalky said, with a vast and macabre satisfaction. 'Wife of a doctor she was'n all, but he got 'imself out of it—blamed the poor ruddy theatre sister, as I remember—'

'Chalky! Chalky!' The rugger playing students were bawling again and Chalky sighed, and said without anger, 'Noisy little baskets. I'll 'ave their guts for garters if they don't bloody belt up. I'll bring yer some sausage rolls when the next lot's ready. They're right good tonight—' and he went away with the swift litheness so many heavy men seem to have.

'Did you hear that?' Barney said, and took hold of Jeff's elbow. 'Did you know that story? I never heard it! The old boy had a death on the table once, and blamed someone else for it! Maybe this time he—'

Jeff shook his head. 'Sorry, old boy. That's not on. That story's been going around for donkey's years—there's always tales of that sort about senior men, you know that. I don't think there's anything in it from your point of view. He did have a death on the table—but it *was* theatre sister's fault. She hadn't supplied the right gear or something, and there was a big bleed, and he hadn't the right stuff to stop it in time. That was all there was to that tale. I'd forget it if I were you—'

Barney subsided again, and Lucy put out a

76

hand, impulsively. He took it, and held on to it, almost absentmindedly.

'Look, both of you,' she said, sounding rather braver than she felt. 'Can't we be practical about this? Think it through properly? There's been two deaths—unnecessary ones. You think they weren't accidents—Barney?'

'It sounds so melodramatic.' He spoke awkwardly. 'But I can't help it. The more I think about it, the more sure I am there's been—something wrong about it all. I think someone's been deliberately up to something—but I don't know what, or how, or why,' he finished helplessly.

'We don't know why, but we know a bit about what and how,' Lucy said. 'Don't we? I've been thinking too. And as I see it, someone wanted to get at Quayle. And succeeded.'

'But where does the sailor come in?' Barney objected.

She smiled at him, a little shyly.

'You've been so upset, you haven't been thinking properly. Isn't it possible that whoever wanted to get at Quayle first thought it could be done through the anaesthetic? Only, the list got changed unexpectedly, and that poor chap got what was meant for Quayle. And next time, whoever it was got at Quayle through the blood.'

Barney was sitting very straight now, looking at her with eyes brighter than they had

77

been all day.

'You're suggesting murder,' he said bluntly.

'That's right,' Lucy said. 'Why be mealy mouthed about it? Murder. It happens, doesn't it? Someone in the hospital wanted to kill Quayle, and made sure of it.'

'But why?' Jeff too was looking more animated. 'It sounds melodramatic to me too—unless you can say *why*.'

Lucy shrugged. 'I don't know. We're trying to find out, aren't we? I suppose if we check up on Quayle, who he was, and all, we'll find out why. And find out why and—'

'—we'll find out who,' Barney finished.

'Yes,' Lucy said, and then, suddenly aware of the way Barney was holding on to her hand with both of his, extricated it, and sat back, a little pink again at her own rather surprising temerity. It wasn't like her to hold the floor as she had been doing.

'Lucy, I think you're right!' Barney spoke excitedly, raising his voice a little. He had to, because the insistent sickening squeal of an ambulance outside was filling the air with its raucous clamour. 'Look, let's go over now to records and check on this bloke—oh, and find that blood bottle too, and have a look at the way it matches up with another bottle of Group A, and then we can go to Stroud and insist he calls the police—'

Another squealing siren joined the first, and then another, and Jeff looked round. People

78

were going over to the door, staring out across the road to the hospital.

'There must have been one hell of a smash-up somewhere to bring that many ambulances in,' he shouted above the noise. 'What do you suppose—'

Barney was on his feet, and hurrying across to the door, pushing through the crowd. And then he looked back over his shoulder, his face suddenly white.

'They're not ambulances—they're fire engines!' he shouted. 'Over at the hospital—come on!'

And grabbing Lucy's hand as she hurried over to him, he plunged through the crowd, pulling her after him, into the lurid light in the street beyond as yet another engine came shrieking hysterically round the corner.

CHAPTER SIX

They became aware of it as soon as they were out of the 'Ship and Bottle', the thick throat-tearing acrid smell of smoke. Lucy, running behind Barney through the crowd of gawping watchers who seemed to have appeared from nowhere, who might almost have crawled out of the cracks of the pavements where they had been waiting for some disaster like this to enjoy, thought confusedly of Mrs Chester, and

79

Miss Symington in the next bed, and the others of her patients who were heavy and helpless. Would the night nurses on duty be able to cope with fire drill, be able to get all the patients out safely? Fire. She was filled with sick terror. The one disaster that every hospital fears above all others, and now it was happening at the Royal, her own Royal.

Barney pushed people aside with scant regard for politeness, leaving a wake of ''Ere! Watch it, mate!' and 'stop yer shoving!' and similar comments behind them, and Lucy willy-nilly followed him, held as she was by the wrist.

They dodged yet another fire engine that came rattling and roaring and squealing past them through the Casualty entrance, ran round the corner and into the main courtyard and stopped. And breathed, almost in unison, a deep sigh of relief.

The main ward block stood serene and solid, as uncompromisingly black as ever, with the dim squares of its windows showing the silhouettes of heads where nurses and patients peered curiously out to see what was happening. But there was no sign of fire anywhere on its seven floors.

Lucy turned, trying to tell from whence the noise and smell of smoke was coming, and then saw the glow high above the roof of the Nurses' Home. At least none of the patients were in danger then, for the Private Block too was quiet, and stood well clear of the area in which the fire seemed to be.

But nurses might be in danger. There were two hundred girls living in that building, and it was reasonable to suppose that at least a hundred of them were in it right now, for it was past ten o'clock, and junior nurses weren't allowed out after half past ten anyway.

Lucy felt sick as she thought of the building, of the way it was hemmed in by the administrative office block and the Path lab and Pharmacy, of the narrow iron fire escapes that twisted round the face of the building and the way it alarmed one to use them even for a practice. And now it was the real thing.

It was her turn now to grab Barney's hand and pull him after her as she ran headlong across the broad courtyard towards the garden and the Nurses' Home. She didn't know why she did it, but she had to keep him with her, couldn't possibly have made her way there alone.

The fire engines were clustered in the consultant's car park, and a part of Lucy's mind registered the fact that Mr Fitzwilliam's car, a rather flashy purple Jaguar, had received a heavy dent in one wing, and was amused. He would be speechless with rage when he saw it.

Thick snakes of swollen hosepipe were twisted along the ground, and the smell of smoke was stronger, as the air seemed to thicken, and people appeared as heavy shadows moving awkwardly in the murk.

Lucy stopped, and pulled back, and Barney put both arms round her from behind, so that she stood in the shelter of his body. And even in her anxiety and the fear that twisted its tendrils through her belly, she felt that familiar lurch of pleasure at his touch.

'Where is it? Can you see?' Barney shouted, for the noise here was considerable, as people shouted and the engines rattled as hose was drawn out and equipment organised.

'Not properly—but it must be the Home,' Lucy shouted back, and then, 'I can't just stand here—there may be girls in there who can't get out—look, I'm going to the Home along the Private Wing lower corridor—are you coming?'

'Yes—' And Barney turned and together they ran across the car park, past the engines and the crowds of people who were standing straining their eyes to see what was happening, and into the small door that led to the Private Wing.

The silence inside came almost as a shock. The corridor that ran the full length of the ground floor—a considerable length for the Private Wing was a long narrow sliver of a building—was silent and deserted. The wall lights were burning on its pale primrose painted walls, their stark Nineteen Thirtyish design repeating to apparent infinity right to the far end, where a tall mirror blocked the way and reflected the corridor back on itself.

'I hope the garden door is unlocked,' Lucy said anxiously, 'though we could get the key from the board in the Porter's Lodge in the entrance hall if it isn't—'

'Lucy—'

She turned her head to look at him, and was startled at the expression on his face. He looked as though he was concentrating on an idea, concentrating hard, yet at the same time there was an element of remoteness in his eyes.

'Yes?' she said, a little puzzled, creasing her forehead.

But all he did was take her face in his hands, cupping her cheeks in his palms, and bent his head and kissed her, gently at first and then more urgently.

And Lucy was so startled that she didn't even close her eyes, found her vision filled with an enormous close up of his eyelids.

And even when he lifted his head, and let go of her she stood quite unmoving, staring upwards in a sort of stupefaction.

'I'm sorry,' Barney said softly. 'But quite suddenly that was the only thing I could possibly do.'

It was like coming to from a faint—or so she imagined, for she had never fainted in her life—and she stood still for a second before speaking. And then was startled at the huskiness of her own voice.

'Don't apologise. I—there's no need to

apologise. Though this is a pretty extraordinary moment to choose—'

'Yes, I know. But I had to. We'll talk about it later. Come on—'

Together they ran along the corridor and Lucy didn't know whether her heart was pounding so heavily because of the physical effort she was making, or because of her fear of the fire, or because of that unexpected, incredible, marvellous moment she had just experienced in Barney's arms.

'You think the garden door might be locked, Lucy?'

'It might—'

'Then we'll take the keys anyway—in case,' Barney said, and then turned right into the square parquet floored hall that led to the main entrance to the Wing.

The Porter's Lodge, a small glassed-in cubicle that contained a small chair, a table, and a tiny three line switchboard, was quiet—clearly the porter on duty had gone to the fire. On the far wall was a tall board, with hooks arranged in rows of six, and on several of the hooks, bunches of keys dangled.

'Which key is it?' Barney asked, and Lucy reached past him for it.

'This one—next to the theatre bunch,' she said quickly and unhooked it, and then they were running again, along the rest of the corridor, to the door at the far end.

But the door was unlocked, and they pushed

84

its heavy panels, and emerged into the garden beyond, and almost reared back as the noise and smell and the livid flickering light hit them.

It was a moment or two before Lucy could make out properly what was going on, so thick was the smoke, and so many were the people whose figures were moving about in its hazy clouds.

But then she could see more easily as a sudden sharp gust of wind swooped across the garden and sent the clouds swirling into patches of clarity. And found tears running down her cheeks, ridiculously, for it wasn't the Nurses' Home that was burning at all. She could see it clearly, see the figures of the Home's occupants craning their heads eagerly out of windows as they stared at the hubbub below, in what was usually their peaceful garden.

It was the Pharmacy that was burning, and burning with a vigorous greedy intensity that lit the sky with a spurious cheerfulness. Clouds of orange yellow smoke lifted and danced above the shallow pitch of the roof, and even as Lucy craned her head to see, there was a heavy crackling roar and part of it caved in.

The crowd shifted and moved again, and then Lucy could see the broad silver pencils of water jets as three hoses, each held by a group of straining shiny jacketed and brass helmeted firemen, worked at the blaze, and then the crowd moved again, as a field of wheat moves when a wind passes over it.

Lucy tried to move forwards, but Barney's grip held her, and she turned her head to speak to him. But just then one figure detached itself from the crowd and came lurching towards them.

'Hey—John—what's the matter?' She heard the sharp note of anxiety in Barney's voice behind her, and peered at the figure in front of her.

It was John Hickson, his usually sleek hair rumpled, and his eyes staring behind his glasses. There was a broad black streak across one cheek, and he stopped, bewildered, and stared at them both.

'What? Oh—Barney—and Sister Beaumont. My God, but this is a mess—'

'How did it start?' Barney shouted above the noise.

'Don't know—I just don't know—' Hickson sounded as bewildered as he looked. 'But it's a mess—and I've had enough. I've got to get away from all this—it's driving me mad—' and indeed he looked ghastly in the uneven light of the flames.

'How long have you been over here?' Barney persisted, and the other man shook his head.

'I don't know—I don't know—' and then he plunged past them, and fumbled with the Private Wing's garden door, and almost fell through it, letting it slam behind him.

'Poor devil—' Barney said. 'He looked

86

terrified—hey, Lucy—where are you going?'

For she had pulled away from him, and was moving towards the burning building, hugging the wall of the laundry block that lay between the Private Wing and the burning Pharmacy.

'I've got to get nearer,' she called back over her shoulder. 'I might be needed—'

'Don't be a fool,' he shouted, moving along beside her, and trying to pull her back. 'Don't be such a bloody little fool!' But she shook her head and moved on, purposefully.

'I've got to. I'm on the accident team—I've got to. If someone is there, and hurt, I'll be needed.'

Immediately he stopped pulling on her shoulder as he had been, and followed her. The specially trained accident teams the hospital provided to send out to disasters like fires and multiple accidents were valuable people, and he knew perfectly well that Lucy might indeed be needed. But even though he wasn't himself trained for one of the teams, he wasn't going to let her go alone into the inferno ahead of them. She had suddenly become a great deal too precious to him for that.

And she was needed. As they reached the small embrasure by the side of the Pharmacy, at the far end of the laundry block, they saw the small knot of people by the wall. Colin Jackson was on his knees beside the prone figure of a fireman, with Harry Caspar beside him as they worked on his inert shape.

'Sister Beaumont—thank God you're here—look, carry on with this man, will you? Artificial respiration. There's another fireman in there and they're trying to get him out—come on, Caspar—'

Barney helped too, and together they worked in grim silence over the still figure of the young fireman. It seemed an eternity passed while they worked, and Lucy was vaguely aware of more shouts from the Pharmacy, more roaring and crackling.

And then, the man under their hands moved, and gasped, and she felt a sudden lift of exhilaration. He was breathing properly, for himself, and she stopped the rhythmic pumping of her arms, and felt the deep ache in her muscles for the first time.

And then a great deal happened at once. The noise from the fire seemed to subside, and though the smoke was still billowing in thick choking clouds, the flames diminished and a darkness spread everywhere. Two men with a stretcher appeared, and with Barney and Lucy's help, shifted the now moaning fireman on to it and took him away. And there were more voices, receding now, as other people moved away from the scene of the fire towards the hospital proper.

Lucy sat back on her heels, aware of the roughness of the ground through the knees of her trousers, and leaned shakily against the wall, and Barney crouched beside her, and put an arm round her, and gratefully she let her head rest on his shoulder. They sat there, side by side on the rough ground, in a sort of numbed weary silence.

A group of people passed them, forming patterns against the sky, and she looked up, almost dreamily, but they didn't seem to notice either her or Barney, down in the shadow of the building, tucked away in their corner.

'I tried to tell you. I tried to, this very afternoon, but you wouldn't see me. And now it's too late, and you'll never be able to find out the truth of it—'

It was a high voice, yet a man's one, and there was an hysterical note in it. Then Stroud's rich plummy voice cut across.

'Tried to tell me what? Pull yourself together, Bruce! Bad enough the place was burned, but at least no one has been badly injured, so there's no need to get into a great panic. Just calm down, will you? Take yourself over to Casualty with the others—someone will give you a sedative no doubt, and then we can sort out matters in the morning when we can see the damage—'

'I tried to tell you—I had the evidence and everything, and now it's gone, all gone, and we'll never know the truth of it—'

'What evidence?' Stroud said irritably. 'I do wish you'd go to Casualty, Bruce—'

'It will be better to listen to Mr Bruce now, Mr Stroud.' It was Colin Jackson's voice, dry

89

and brittle. 'If he's got something to say let him get it out. Otherwise, what with the state of shock he's in, he'll collapse, or something—'

'Well, Bruce?' Stroud's voice was gentler. 'What is it?'

Lucy listened dreamily. It was as though she were an audience at some very realistic play, and as the ache in her arms subsided, and her body relaxed, she burrowed her head more comfortably into Barney's shoulder and listened with a sort of remote interest.

Bruce spoke rapidly, almost gabbling the words.

'I've been puzzled, you see, puzzled for some time. It was amphetamine at first—I couldn't understand why so much was being used, and I checked the ward requisitions, and it was odd, because *they* weren't ordering it. But where was it going to? And it worried me, seeing that amphetamine is one of the drugs the wrong people always want to get their hands on. And I thought about other drugs—morphine and cocaine and heroin, and I began to check up, going through all the drug books as they came in from the wards—only I had to do it slowly. I had to wait till books came in, normally, with requisitions, because it wouldn't do to start a whole hue and cry without real evidence, would it? And then I saw it—saw what had been going on. Someone had been getting large quantities of cocaine and heroin out of the place—it was clever, oh it was clever, I grant you that—but once I'd gone through the books and the records of ordering I could see how it had been done. And I brought all the books over to you, and wanted to show you so that we could deal with it quietly because I knew you wouldn't want the story to get out—I mean, if people found out that we were being robbed of drugs that were worth thousands and thousands of pounds on the illicit drug market, what would it mean to the hospital?—but you wouldn't see me, not at all, and said to come back tomorrow, so I locked the books in the safe in my office and now it's too late and the evidence is all gone and what do we do now?—'

'My God!' Colin Jackson said softly. 'Oh, my God—'

Stroud's voice was strained. 'But the books are surely all right? They must be? Safe? Your office—even if it *is* destroyed the safe will be all right—it was a fireproof one, I know that—'

The little man beside him almost wept. 'But it isn't—it isn't! I mean—it was fireproof, but I got in to try to get the books out safely, and the door was open and the fire was everywhere and the fireman who pulled me out, he said it was obviously where the fire started—'

'It can't be,' Stroud spoke sharply. 'It can't be! It must have started in the sterilising room—you have bunsen burners there and all sorts of inflammable stuff—it *must* have started there—'

'No! No! It started in the office—it started in

91

the safe! Someone did it on purpose, I tell you! Someone found out I was going to tell you, and burned it deliberately! Don't you see? It was the best way to get rid of the evidence against him—and there's something else—there was the hospital's entire supply of heroin and cocaine and amphetamine in that safe—I wasn't taking any more chances, and that's gone too, and who can say whether it was burned, or stolen before the fire started? Whoever's been stealing these drugs—whoever it was, he knew I'd found out, and he did it to get out of trouble—'

Bruce was now frankly weeping. Lucy could hear the sobbing in his voice, and lifted her head, the feeling of remoteness leaving her as she realised the import of what he was saying.

Barney, beside her, seemed to realise at the same time, and quickly pulled her head down again.

'Shhh!' he hissed. 'For God's sake be quiet! I've got to hear this—it may explain—'

'—but who could possibly know what you wanted to tell me?' Stroud was saying. '*I* didn't know—who could have guessed such a thing— who could imagine it could happen here at the Royal? Drugs—oh, my God, it's more than I can cope with—'

Agitation made his voice rise, and Colin Jackson's cut across it like a knife.

'You'd better keep your voice down, Mr Stroud, unless you want the whole damn world to know what's going on. If there was arson here, then the fire people will discover the fact, but until then, Bruce, we'd better say no more—'

'You doctors!' and Bruce's shrill tones showed the hysteria that was in him. 'You doctors! Always stick together—I know you! That's why I wanted to tell Mr Stroud and not the medical staff, because I knew you'd try to cover up—'

'What are you saying?' Jackson's voice was as sharp as a whiplash.

'It was a doctor who did it—or maybe a senior nurse! Someone with access to the ward drug books, *and* the dispensary—only someone with the special knowledge senior staff have could have done it! That's why I wanted to tell Mr Stroud privately tonight, only he wouldn't listen to me—'

'But no one knew you wanted to see me!' Mr Stroud cried. 'No one knew—or—oh, my God!'

'Yes,' Jackson said dryly. 'Your secretary came into your office and said Mr Bruce wanted to see you urgently, remember? And you sent her to tell him to go away and come back in the morning—'

'Oh, my God,' Stroud said again, helplessly, and Lucy, sitting rigid in the shadows, turned her head and stared at Barney in the darkness, her weariness and aches quite gone as she tried to fit this newest piece of information into the kaleidoscope of odd happenings the day had brought.

CHAPTER SEVEN

Lucy sat curled up in one of the wheelchairs in Casualty waiting room, her hands crooked round a mug of hot Ovaltine.

The worst of the hubbub had subsided. The firemen were gone (apart from one who had been admitted to Male Medical with severe respiratory embarrassment due to inhaled smoke), and Mr Bruce, in an almost comatose state, had been tucked into bed in the Private Wing to sleep off the horror of the night.

Beside her, on one of the benches, Jeff Heath and Barney were also drinking Ovaltine gratefully. Jeff's face was strained and dirty, and Lucy grinned at him as he looked up and caught her eye.

'I thought you were right behind us when we ran out of the "Ship in Bottle"', she said apologetically. 'I'm truly sorry to have alarmed you.'

'Hmmph!' Jeff grunted. 'Of course it alarmed me! One minute we're talking and the next you both disappear into a cloud of smoke. For all I knew you could have burnt yourselves to a crisp, rushing off like that—'

'I'm sorry,' Lucy said again, and stilled the

little voice inside that whispered at her, 'No, you're not. If he'd been with you, Barney wouldn't have kissed you, would he? And that was—'

But she refused to think about how that kiss had made her feel. And anyway, it all seemed so odd and absurd now that part of her didn't really believe it had happened at all; thought that it was a mad fantasy born of the wish that it would.

'Jeff,' Barney said abruptly. 'Something happened tonight—'

Jeff threw back his head and laughed harshly. 'Something happened! There's the understatement of the year!'

Barney shook his head impatiently. 'No. I mean—Lucy and I, we overheard something that's almost incredible—but it must be part of this mess we're in—'

Jeff sobered immediately and looked more alert, his eyes narrowing.

'What? Something to do with those patients' deaths?'

'Yes—it must be. Listen—'

'No, Barney!' Lucy hardly knew that she had spoken so sharply, until both men jumped and looked round at her. 'Not here,' she said more gently. 'It's—well, it isn't something to talk about in a public sort of place. You know quite well that *they* wouldn't have said anything if they'd known we were there.'

She looked round the Casualty waiting

95

room, where two or three people still sat. 'Can't we wait to talk about it when we're quiet somewhere?'

'I suppose you're right,' Barney said a little unwillingly, 'though I imagine Jeff will be as interested as I was—'

The double doors that led to the main part of the hospital, via the outpatient department, swung and flapped their rubber edges, and Stroud came through with three other men, one of whom was in the uniform of a senior fire officer, the other two wearing sober dark suits and rather grubby buff coloured mackintoshes.

'Plain clothes police?' Barney breathed softly, staring at them, and Jeff whirled and stared too.

Stroud saw them, and hesitated for a moment. Then he said something to one of the men, who looked sharply at the little group in the corner. Then they crossed the waiting room.

'Ah—erm—Dr Elliot—Dr Heath—I hadn't intended to say much about this at this stage, but since you are both here, there seems little point in delaying. Er—' He seemed embarrassed, and coughed sharply before going on.

'The fact is, as a result of—er—something else that happened here tonight—and you may as well know what it is now as later, I suppose—as a result of the fire, which does not

96

appear to—to have been *entirely* an accident—
matters need investigating. Not only the fire,
you understand, but the other business—the
one we were discussing this afternoon.'

'The murdered patients,' Barney said baldly,
and Stroud looked intensely uncomfortable
and coughed again.

'You think they were murdered?' The taller
of the two men in raincoats spoke sharply in a
flat London voice that just stopped short of
being cockney.

Barney looked briefly at Jeff and Lucy and
nodded crisply.

'We all do. We've been talking about it.'

'Oh, I do wish you wouldn't—really you
should *not* gossip about such matters!' Stroud
said distressfully, and Barney raised his
eyebrows at him.

'Hardly gossip, when both Heath and I
appear to have been involved!'

'They'll have to talk about it, Mr Stroud,'
the tall man said, easily. 'Like it or not, there's
going to be a lot of talk. I'm goin' to encourage
it, too, since that's the best way of finding out
what's what. Now, Dr—Elliot, is it? My name
is Spain, Detective Inspector Joseph Spain.
This is Detective Sergeant Travers. Quite a day
you've had here today, hmm?'

'Two deaths and a fire,' Jeff grunted. 'You
could call it quite a day, I suppose.'

'Ah, yes, you'll be Dr Heath. How d'y'do. As
I understand it, both of you have something to
97

contribute to any investigations I make, so I'll be wanting to talk to both of you—'

Inspector Spain looked at Lucy then and smiled. It was an attractive smile, lifting his rather heavy face into a friendly expression.

'And who might this young lady be? One of these gentlemen's girl friends?'

'I'm Sister Beaumont,' Lucy said, with considerable dignity.

The smile broadened. 'Really? Who'd have thought it? You don't look the sort of battleaxe I imagined sisters to be.'

Lucy reddened. Had she realised just how young she looked, with her hair ruffled and her round face smudged with dirt, she might have been less annoyed at Spain's attitude.

'Do you know much about what's been going on here?' Spain went on.

'Only what Barney—Dr Elliot has told me,' Lucy said, and Inspector Spain nodded.

'I see. Well, that's interesting too. Always useful to know who's on whose side, as it were. Helps sort out the information we collect, doesn't it, Travers?' And Lucy blushed furiously again at Travers' knowing grin.

'Are you going to start your investigations tonight—er—this morning?' Stroud cut in, a little irritably, looking up at the big clock above them. 'It's almost one o'clock you know, and it's been a long day—'

'Indeed it has,' Inspector Spain said equably. 'I've been working too, believe it or

98

not. No, not now. We'll need daylight to have a good look at that Pharmacy and work out what's what, won't we? What I'd like to suggest is a meeting with you gentlemen—and anyone else involved—at around nine o'clock. I'll start in the Pharmacy at six-thirty or thereabouts. I'll be glad if you can be there then, if you please, Mr Stroud.' He glanced a little maliciously at Stroud, whose face had fallen ludicrously, and then grinned again as he turned away.

Then he stopped, and looked back at Lucy. 'You come too, Sister. If you've been discussing this business with your—friends— we'll maybe glad of your contributions as an onlooker, as it were. Yes. See you at nine, then. Good morning!'

It was another half hour before Lucy went over to the Nurses' Home to bed, with Barney escorting her across the courtyard. Jeff had insisted on knowing what they had heard at the scene of the fire, and since the waiting room was by then empty of people, Lucy had not demurred, although she was desperately tired and longing to go to bed. But Jeff had gone up to the doctors' quarters at last, and Barney had insisted on seeing Lucy safely to the Home before going to bed himself.

'Though what could happen between here and the Home, I can't imagine—' Lucy said, trying to pretend she didn't particularly want him to accompany her. But Barney just smiled down at her and tucked her hand into the crook of his elbow.

They stood a little awkwardly at the door of the Nurses' Home, in the still lingering smokiness, staring across at the wrecked Pharmacy building at the far end of the garden. And then suddenly Barney ducked his head, and kissed her cheek, holding her shoulders in a firm grip, before saying softly, 'Goodnight, Lucy.'

'Goodnight,' she whispered, looking up at him in the darkness, wishing he'd kissed her properly. 'I—I'll see you in the morning then?'

'Yes—' He still stood there, and there was a moment's silence. Then he said, almost whispering himself, 'Thank you for being so nice tonight, Lucy. I don't know what I'd have done if you hadn't been around.'

And then he chuckled softly. 'This was one hell of a first date, wasn't it? Next time, we'll have a less—strenuous time, I promise. Yes? We'll go out somewhere together, properly.'

'I'd like that,' Lucy said, and suddenly aware that if she didn't go she would almost certainly throw her arms round him and kiss him herself, she turned, and slipped in through the big doors, leaving Barney to take himself back to the main block and the doctors' quarters in a dreamlike state composed of fatigue and anxiety and an extraordinary sense of elation which was, he thought, quite ridiculous under the circumstances.

In the broad light of the following morning, the sense of elation had subsided, but it left a deep warm glow that helped him to face breakfast in the doctors' dining room with far more equanimity than he would have thought possible.

Not that breakfast was a particularly pleasant meal. Jeff sat and glowered but then Jeff tended to be a glum sort of man at the best of times, and the others were strained and silent as Barney came in and helped himself to scrambled eggs and toast.

'Any further developments?' he asked Colin Jackson, who was barricaded behind the *Telegraph*.

'What sort of developments do you want?' Colin said harshly. 'Haven't we had enough to satisfy you?' He looked at Barney with an expression almost of dislike, and suddenly dropped his paper and leaned forwards.

'I'll tell you this much, Elliot, and I'll tell Heath too. In my estimation there's been a great deal of hot air talked around here. Two patients died under strange circumstances, I know—but they aren't *that* strange. It could still be due to plain old fashioned negligence, and I for one am not going to be swept off my feet by a lot of dramatic talk about murders. Talk like that could be a very useful smokescreen—'

'What the hell are you getting at?' Barney felt his face whiten.

101

'Just what I say. Until I see the result of the post mortems I'm not going to go around saying "poor devils" about either of you. Murder! For God's sake, *why*? And more to the point, *how*? Tell me how that poor bastard of a sailor died, and show me that it was nothing to do with the anaesthetic you gave and maybe I'll listen to talk about killing—but until you can show me facts like that, I'll stick to my own ideas. And you might as well know it—'

'Be quiet, Colin.' This was Cantrell, enjoying an early breakfast at the hospital's expense, although as a married man he was non-resident. An even tempered person, rather older than the average for anaesthetic registrars, he was the only man in the room approaching Colin Jackson in seniority, and so the only one really able to talk to him on equal terms.

'You know as well as I do that Barney is in one hell of an equivocal position. To actually *prove* a conclusive cause of death in a case like this is bloody nearly impossible. I don't blame him for seizing on the possibility there's been— what do the police call it?—foul play? yes, foul play. I'd think the same thing in his position, damned if I wouldn't—'

Barney had had a chance to simmer down from the rush of fury Colin's icy disbelief had aroused in him, and thinking about what Colin had said, had to admit in all fairness that he

102

had made a point.

How had the sailor died? He had arrived in theatre, a man in good general condition with a well defined surgical emergency condition, and no more. The operation had gone perfectly smoothly up until the point at which the pulse had begun to fail, and there could not for one moment be any possibility that the operative procedures had caused his death. It had undoubtedly been something to do with his anaesthetic. And Barney Elliot had given that anaesthetic.

The glow with which he had started the day diminished, flickered as he thought of Lucy and wondered whether she had had any bright ideas about it all, and then finally died when Jackson spoke again.

'Oh, I don't blame him for making the most of such excuses as he can. I'm just saying I see them for what they are—excuses. Bad enough we had the deaths here, without the place being littered up with police. A little less noisy talk would have avoided *them*, and the upheaval and talk they'll cause—'

'Like hell it would,' Barney said swiftly. 'As I understand it, from what Inspector Spain said last night, they were called in because of the fire—because of the drug business.'

Jackson raised his head sharply. 'Now, how do you know about that?' he said softly.

Barney could have kicked himself. He and Lucy hadn't deliberately listened in to the conversation Jackson and Stroud and Bruce had had last night, but all the same, it wasn't pleasant to admit to eavesdropping.

'I heard you,' he said sulkily, after a moment. 'Last night. Outside the Pharmacy. And if it's true, then it seems reasonable to suppose that those deaths were in some way linked. You'd hardly get two different criminals at work in the same place at the same time.'

'As I've already pointed out, there's a good deal of doubt, in my mind at any rate, that there was anything criminal about those deaths anyway. I find the fact you know that last night's fire was probably caused deliberately very significant—'

'Deliberately? What's that?' John Hickson spoke for the first time, and Barney turned and looked at him. His face was extraordinarily pale.

Jackson stood up and made for the door. 'You'll all find out soon enough, I suppose,' he said curtly. 'There is evidence to suggest the fire was due to arson. The police have been over there since the crack of dawn, poking about, and I've already talked to Spain. *He* regards the evidence as conclusive. And Bruce is convinced that the arsonist was trying to cover up some drug stealing that had been going on. You'll all be interviewed some time today, I gather—so how the hell I'm to keep the hospital working, God only knows! I must tell you, Elliot, that I have every intention of informing Spain that you knew about the fact it was arson before I told you. Good morning,' and he went, slamming the door behind him.

Barney swore loudly and fluently, and Jeff leaned back in his chair and said flatly, 'Shut up, Barney. You've got nothing to worry about.'

'Nothing to worry about? With that—that sanctimonious devil after my blood? Not much!'

'Oh, of course you haven't!' Jeff said impatiently. 'You've got a witness, haven't you? Lucy was with you. And you've got me. You began to tell me about it *before* Stroud spoke to us last night and told us officially. Simmer down, man.'

Jeff turned his head then, and looked very directly at Hickson.

'What interests me, Hickson, is why you're so agitated about all this. You looked sick when Jackson mentioned arson. Why? Are you involved in this mess by any chance?'

'Me—What? Of course not. Not at all. I'm just—I didn't like—I mean, it's a horrible thought, isn't—?' Hickson was floundering badly, and his face was a sick greenish white as he got to his feet and made clumsily for the door. 'The whole business is—just too horrible—' and he too slammed the door behind him.

'That's odd,' Barney said, staring after him.

105

'You're right, Jeff. Why the hell is *he* in such a state? He looked like that last night, too—'

'Last night?' Jeff said quickly.

'Mmm. At the fire. He came past us looking like death—really bothered. Do you suppose—no, it couldn't be! Not that little wet—'

'I don't know. It could be anyone!' Jeff said, showing some real animation for once. 'Isn't that the point Bruce made? Or so you said. It had to be a doctor—or perhaps a senior nurse—who meddled with the drug requisitions—why not Hickson?'

'My God, this is horrible!' Harry Caspar too made for the door, looking sick. 'Is this what's going to be going on here from now on? Everyone accusing everyone else, suspecting everyone else? It'll be hell—'

'That's exactly what it'll be like,' Derek Foster said bitterly. 'Exactly. I've already been talked at by those lousy police—'

'What? You didn't tell us!' Barney said.

'I haven't had much of a chance,' Derek snapped. 'You've all been talking your flamin' heads off. They copped me at seven o'clock, on my way in this morning—'

'You were out last night? All night?' Jeff asked quickly.

Derek grinned. 'I was, pal, I was. I've got to get my love life in some time—'

'Can you prove you were out all night?' Barney asked. 'Because if you can you're in the clear. I imagine the police are going to want to know where everyone was last night, when the fire started, I mean—'

'They do,' Derek said. 'I've already been asked that. And seein' I've no old fashioned notions about protecting women's names, I've satisfied 'em already. Well, up to a point. They still had a lot more questions to ask about that Polish sailor—'

There was a tap at the door, and Sheila, the red headed maid, put her head round it, and said breathlessly, 'Inspector Spain's compliments and would Dr Elliot and Dr Heath be so good as to remember the appointment he made with them last night, for which they are already late, and he's waitin' over in the Pharmacy for youse both, and will Mr Foster please go too, he says.'

They walked over to the Pharmacy in silence, each busy with his own thoughts. Barney's were in a turmoil. As Harry had said, it was hell to find himself looking at each of his colleagues with a suspicious eye, but under the circumstances, it was impossible not to.

Why is Colin Jackson so adamant in his belief Jeff and I were negligent? Is it because he's trying to cover himself in some way? Why did John Hickson look so sick about it all, and what was he doing last night at the Pharmacy to make him look so extraordinary when he pushed by us? Why was Derek Foster at such pains to tell us he was out last night? To make

107

an alibi for himself? Is it because really he was here, and started the fire?

And come to think of it, what about those deaths and the part Sir James played in them? Was Chalky White telling us something important last night when he told us about the time a patient of Sir James' died on the table?

And then there's the nursing staff—did Staff Nurse Cooper really lock the anaesthetic room that night, or was she just creating a diversion in making such a fuss about it all?

By the time they reached the Pharmacy, Barney couldn't think clearly at all. Indeed, he was so confused by his own thoughts that for a few moments he didn't even notice Lucy was already there, looking crisp and fresh in her navy and white uniform, her hair curling prettily round her starched lace scrap of a cap. But she saw him immediately and felt good. No matter what happened, she was discovering, life was a pretty colourless business if Barney Elliot wasn't around. And when he was, she could cope with anything—even the unhappy anxiety in his face. And she moved over to stand beside him in the burnt out shell of the main dispensing room, caring not a whit for the faintly raised eye-brows of Sister Osgood, who watched her closely.

They were all there, all the people who had been in Stroud's office the previous day, even Sir James, but with the addition of John Hickson and Derek Foster, Mr Bruce, who was sitting perched awkwardly on a pile of dusty masonry and looking rather ill, and Mr Stroud's secretary, whose thin face was agog with interest. She was the only person who seemed to be gaining any pleasure from the situation, with the exception of Inspector Spain, who turned from poking in the twisted metal shell of the safe as the three doctors arrived. He grinned agreeably at them.

'Ah, you got here at last, then. Good. Now, seein' I've got you all rounded up, let's see if I can get some sense out of this strange situation, shall I? I don't suppose it'll take me that long—not if you co-operate. Only I'll tell you one thing before we start. I've got a nose for lies—a real nose. Even if you bend the truth only a little bit, I'll spot it, because that's my job, eh Travers? Just like you lot spot a real illness, no matter what the patient may choose to say. So let's save all our time, and tell the truth, eh? Good. I'll start with yesterday morning's operations, then—'

CHAPTER EIGHT

Watching and listening carefully, Lucy thought, '—he's enjoying this. He's like a puppet master making us all dance when he tells us to. Only we're talking instead of dancing.'

109

And suddenly she found Spain's relaxed urbanity somehow sinister, as she listened to Hickson stammering and stuttering through an explanation of why he was in the theatres during the sailor's operation, and shrank nearer to Barney's comforting bulk. And then realised she had done it, and moved back a step again to stand with her hands primly folded on her apron front.

Barney, too, had been a little repelled by Spain's smooth handling of this difficult group of people, by the quiet way Sergeant Travers' pencil slid over the pages of his shorthand notebook, but gradually his interest in what was going on rose to the top, and he listened intently.

And then, suddenly, the talking stopped, as Spain turned to Travers and held out his hand for the notebook. The two policemen stood with their heads together as Spain read swiftly through the squiggle-covered pages, and the hospital people moved and rustled, but didn't speak, avoiding looking at each other's faces. Even Sir James seemed somehow discomfited, and stood leaning against a charred wall with his heavy face closed and lowering.

'Well, now,' Spain's voice made them jump slightly. 'I think I begin to see a little light in this. Only a little, mind you, but enough to sort out fact from surmise. So let's look at what we've got.'

He sat himself on the remains of the safe,

and beamed round at them. 'I know this isn't the most comfortable place to be in, but bear with me, and I'll let you all get back to your important work as soon as possible. Now. Since yesterday morning, two parts of this hospital seem to have been involved in some unexpected goings on. The theatres first—the Private Wing Theatres. Two patients died there.

'Now, the first patient died as a result of his anaesthetic. Of that much we can be fairly certain, even though we haven't yet got the findings of the post mortem. Nasty things, post mortems.' He shuddered with a faintly theatrical air. 'Yes, nasty. Now, the doctor who gave the anaesthetic tells us he thinks his patient was murdered. He can't tell us how, or why, or anything nice and solid like that. Just that he believes it.'

Barney reddened painfully and opened his mouth to speak, but Spain went on unhurriedly, yet with an authority that effectively overrode Barney's attempt.

'And then there was the second patient. He died *after* his operation, as the result of being given a blood transfusion that was started in the operating theatres. Now, stop me if I get these difficult medical facts wrong—' and he smiled to show that he knew perfectly well that he wouldn't '—but as I understand it, people have to have blood specially chosen for them. A bottleful has to be specially matched to the

111

patient's own blood, because if the wrong blood is given, it can kill. Mr Heath tells us he *did* match the blood properly but that somehow the wrong blood got into the bottle between the time he crossmatched it and the time it was given to that poor ill man.' His face sketched sympathy for the dead Quayle, and he lifted limpid eyes to Jeff's face, which in its turn showed ugly red blotches. But Jeff's attempts to speak were also overridden by the equable Spain.

'Bottles of blood come to this hospital from the blood transfusion centre, already labelled as to group. All that has to be done here is to select the right group, match it, and label it with the patient's name. Dr Heath said he did this. Sir James and Mr Caspar tell us that when they checked, it was the wrong blood, even though the bottle bore Quayle's name. We can't do any checking back on this, with the transfusion centre, owing to the fact that Sister Palmer who was in charge of Quayle's ward didn't return the bottle unwashed to the laboratory as she should have done. The bottle was returned after having been carefully sluiced out.'

Sister Palmer looked desperately distressed. 'I told you!' she burst out. 'I told you! It was a new junior nurse! She forgot all she'd been told about blood transfusions and the stupid creature washed the bottle. I *told* you—'

'Yes, Sister. I know you did! Everyone's

tellin' me everything,' Spain said with wide-eyed innocence. 'All I'm doin' now is running a brief outline of what happened. So, as I say, we can't prove Dr Heath isn't to blame, any more than we can prove Dr Elliot isn't to blame for what happened to *his* patient. But they both agree that murder has been done. Once more, Dr Heath can't tell us why or how—how the wrong blood was given, that is, though we accept that it was.'

Jeff didn't attempt to speak. He just stood with his arms folded and looked directly at Spain with a twist to his mouth that showed a fine disdain. Spain didn't seem to notice.

'So, there we have a few facts and a hell of a lot of surmise. Yes, lots of surmise. But now we come to what I like best—*solid* facts. Yesterday afternoon Mr Bruce took himself off to Mr Stroud's office to report his discovery of a series of very clever thefts of drugs—drugs that bring a big price on the illicit market. Amphetamine—black bombers, and the like. Heroin. And snow—cocaine. When he got to Stroud's office, he met Dr Hickson outside, and in his efforts to avoid letting Dr Hickson see that he was carrying all the drug requisition books managed to drop some, which Dr Hickson picked up and gave back to him. I mention this—' Spain looked directly at Hickson, who looked even sicker than he had that morning, '—to show that he knew, in common with everyone else here, that Mr

113

Bruce wanted to see Mr Stroud on an important matter. The rest of you knew because Mr Stroud's secretary came into the office where you all were and announced the fact.

'Right. We now move on to late last night. The Pharmacy started to burn. It was assumed that the fire had started in the sterilising room, which in fact is almost undamaged. It was the most likely place for a truly accidental fire to start, because of its bunsen burners and sterilisers and what have you, so it was a natural assumption. Well, unfortunately for someone, the fire was admirably controlled by our noble friends in the fire service—' and Spain produced a bland smile, '—and a good look around this morning confirms last night's suspicions. The fire was deliberately started by someone pouring paraffin over the drug books which Mr Bruce had put in there, after Mr Stroud had refused to see him—' Stroud shifted his feet miserably, '—and that someone also removed the entire stock of amphetamine, heroin and cocaine which Mr Bruce had prudently locked in there with the books. Not all that prudently, as it turns out.

'And this brings me to another point. In talking to you all this morning, I've been shocked—' he produced a prim expression '—shocked to discover just how casual you hospital people are about keys. You lock up important places when you leave them

114

unattended, and then go and hang the keys on boards where any Tom, Dick or Harry can help himself to them!'

'We've told you why!' Stroud burst out. 'We keep on telling you. A hospital gives a twenty-four hour service! We've got to be able to get to every part of the hospital at any time, without having to dig out some individual who has the keys! Bruce lives right out in the suburbs! If we needed some urgent drug in the middle of the night, it would take hours to get it! So, the dispensary keys hang on the board in the doctors' common room when Bruce is away from the building, so that any doctor who needs them can get to them—and it's the same with the laboratory keys and the operating theatre keys—only they, the Private Wing Theatre keys, hang on the board in the porter's lodge in the Private Wing—'

Spain opened his eyes very wide. 'I know you told me why!' he said. 'But I'm still shocked! There must be a better way of ensuring security—'

'We aren't bloody policemen,' Jeff said and his voice was grating. 'We're doctors. We're more concerned with giving the patients immediate care when they need it than with *security*.'

'Yes,' Spain said smoothly. 'Quite. Which brings me to my last point. Any one of you doctors could have got into this Pharmacy last night, and set it on its merry burnin' way. Any

115

one of you that had a motive. Mr Bruce has given us information that suggests what that motive is. What we know about the way Mr Bruce came over to Mr Stroud's office last night shows that you were all warned that there was urgent reason to do something to cover up those thefts. What we know about the keys tells us that you all had equal opportunity. So you see, we've got a lovely lot of facts. Seven doctors. Four nurses. Three administrative staff. Anyone of you could have been the drug thief, because you all had fair warning that the thefts were about to be revealed.'

He looked round consideringly. 'We can cut out Mr Bruce, since he was goin' to do the revealing.' Mr Bruce produced a twisted smile. 'We can cut out Mr Stroud and his secretary, since they lack the specialist medical knowledge necessary to cook the drug books— which Mr Bruce assures us was cleverly done. We'll have to take his word for it, seein' the books are no longer in the world of the livin'. So what are we left with? Doctors, Jackson, Foster, Caspar, Hickson, Heath, Elliot and Sir James—'

Dispassionately he let his glance move from one to the other, as he said their names, and they each responded in their special ways, Jackson looking disdainful, Derek Foster, Harry Caspar and John Hickson deeply embarrassed in varying degrees, and Jeff and Barney plain angry. Sir James was the only one

116

who just stared back at the policeman impassively.

'Of course,' Inspector Spain went on. 'There's still the ladies—our four charmin' nurses. Sister Osgood and Sister Palmer and Nurse Cooper were all in Mr Stroud's office yesterday, and all have the necessary understanding of the drug requisitioning system that would make the thefts possible. Sister Beaumont, on the other hand—' Lucy felt her face whiten as Spain's considering glance took her in. 'Sister Beaumont is Dr Elliot's girl, and spent the evenin' with him. *If*—and I'm only sayin' *if*—Dr Elliot is involved, I think it's reasonable to suppose his girl friend is too. So you must join the ranks of suspects, Sister—'

Lucy wanted to die, quietly and immediately. She could feel the eyes of the other two Sisters fixed disapprovingly on her, was aware of sharp glances from Jackson and Stroud, but above all was aware of Barney standing beside her. Spain had no right to say such things, to stampede them into such a situation, calling her Barney's 'girl friend'! It was too much to cope with, too—

And then Barney took her hand in his and held it tightly and said loudly, 'That is bloody outrageous! How dare you suggest that Sister Beaumont would—'

'Oh, Dr Elliot!' Spain said, and his voice was exaggeratedly patient. 'I'm a policeman! We're trained to be outrageous, just like you're trained to save lives! I can say what I like, you know, while I'm investigatin' and no one can do a thing about it. But don't you fret yourself, Doctor. I'm not gunnin' for your Sister Beaumont—she looks too nice to be involved with anythin' sordid, doesn't she? Yes. I was just pointin' out why I got you all here this morning. Because you're all in some way connected with what's goin' on—'

He paused, and then looked round at the group again.

'So. Some hard facts—proven arson, and virtually proven drug runnin'. Some wild surmises, like Stout Cortes' lot went in for, about murders. Well, I'm lookin' into those deaths very carefully. If I find the facts that *prove* them to be murders, I won't be a bit surprised, mind you. In my experience where drugs are involved murder and God knows what else isn't far in the background.'

His voice hardened and for the first time the bantering note left it and he spoke with very real feeling.

'If there's one thing that makes me sick it's drug runnin'. I pity the poor bastards that use the stuff—you'll never find *me* hounding poor bloody addicts to desperation—but I *hate* the people who supply them. So I give you fair warning, whoever you are—and it should be clear enough to all of you that it's got to be one of you—I give you fair warning that I'm after

118

your guts. And I'll get you. Right. I'm now goin' over to the admin. block where I've been given an office to use. If anyone has anything they want to tell me, they can come at any time to speak to me or Sergeant Travers. Good morning.'

And he pulled his coat around his heavy body and walked swiftly out of the Pharmacy block, turning right into the covered way that led to the Administrative offices, leaving them sullenly staring after him.

The group broke up, going back uneasily to work, without talking very much to each other. Inspector Spain seemed to have wrung them dry, and his final clear warning had alarmed them all. As Barney said, as he and Lucy walked across the garden towards the hospital, 'It doesn't matter how clear a conscience you've got, whenever accusations get thrown around, you immediately get all red and hot and look guilty—'

As they passed the big copper beech tree in the middle of the garden, Barney suddenly seized her wrist, and pulled her into its shadows, making her sit down on the wooden seat that was built round its heavy trunk.

'Barney!' she protested, but not with any great conviction. 'For heaven's sake! I've got to get on duty! The morning's half gone, as it is—'

'Then ten minutes either way won't make all that much difference. Listen, Lucy—' and then

119

he stopped and just stared at her.

'Yes?' she said softly.

'There are little yellow bits in your eyes.' He sounded surprised.

'I prefer to call them amber flecks,' she said, and her voice was uneven. 'It sounds more interesting. I—It's just a genetic accident, really. My mother had amber coloured eyes, and Dad's were brown, so I've got a mixture—'

'You talk too much,' he said, and kissed her lips very softly.

'Barney! Have some sense! Broad daylight, in the nurses' garden! Are you demented? You'll have me drummed out. You know what an old bag Matron is. She goes mad if she finds out medical staff are within spitting distance of the Nurses' Home—and you go around kissing me right under her windows—'

'She'll be over in her office now, so who cares?' Barney said, and kissed her again, and Lucy lifted her face and co-operated with a great deal of enthusiasm.

'Listen, Lucy,' he said when he had raised his head from hers, rather unwillingly. 'I wanted to tell you—I'm sorry about what Spain said just now. About your being my girl friend, I mean. Damn and blast! That isn't what I mean at all. I'm not complaining because he called you my girl friend, but because it was there, with those gawping idiots, and—'

'I know,' she said gently. 'It's all right.'

'Is it? Really? I was—afraid. Afraid you'd

get all prickly and sheer off me, or something.'

'I'm not the prickly kind,' Lucy said.

'No.' He reached out his hand and touched her face gently, running the tips of his fingers along the curve of her lips. 'No. Not prickly.'

'Barney—if you don't let me go on duty, I—I can't answer for the consequences.' She laughed a little breathlessly. 'Please? Can't we—er—continue this conversation some other time?'

'Would you like that? To continue this specific conversation?'

She took a deep breath, and then nodded. 'Yes, I would. Very much.' And then grinned a little ruefully. 'Oh, Lor! How's that for a declaration?'

'If that's what it was, it's just fine!' and he stood up, and held out both hands to pull her to her feet. 'It's the best thing I've heard this morning. *Nice* Lucy—' and he bent his head to kiss her again, and then they walked in companionable silence, each glowing with an absurd pink and white happiness, across to the hospital.

He came to the ward with her. 'I might just as well,' he pointed out, when she demurred. 'Seeing I can't do any work. I've got to have Cantrell to hold my hand all the time, so he might just as well work alone as with me. I've nothing else to do. Can't I come to the ward?'

And he looked so pathetically at her, that she laughed, and agreed, for of course there

121

was nothing she wanted more than to have him with her all the time.

He sat peaceably in her office, drinking coffee and watching her as she checked the report book, and the requisitions, and took control of the day's work. And sat on until lunch-time while she moved about the ward dealing with medicine rounds, and treatments, and ward visits from the physicians.

And all the time he sat, he thought and thought, trying to make some sense out of what Spain had discovered, and above all, to make some sense out of the deaths of the previous day.

It was after lunch—which they took together in her office, sharing egg sandwiches and soup—that it happened.

Staff Nurse Crowther put her head round the office door just before two to announce the imminent arrival of a new admission. 'She's in a diabetic coma, Sister?' she said, 'Casualty said could we please prepare a tray to give plain insulin intravenously. Forty units IV, and then sixty intradermally. And they want a drip—'

'They're sure it's a diabetic coma, and not an insulin one?' Lucy asked, getting up swiftly and moving over to the drug cupboard. 'I remember the last case they sent up, and she was in insulin coma—sweating heavily— though the GP had said it was a diabetic coma.'

'No, Sister, I specially checked.' Nurse Crowther grinned. 'Sister in casualty chewed my ears off for asking. Thought I was criticising *her*—this one's as dry as they come, and there's no doubt about it being a diabetic coma—'

'All right. Prepare a bed and a tray, will you? I'll bring the insulin.'

She dug in her pockets for her keys, and Barney leaned back, his hands in the pockets of his own white coat, and watched her. Just looking at her, at the shape of her firm round body under the starch of her uniform made him feel good. Then he swore softly, and pulled his hand out of his pocket.

'What's the matter?' Lucy had found her keys, and turned to look at him anxiously.

'It's all right—I've sliced my finger, I've got a stupid habit—will put empty ampoules in my pockets. It's safer, really—stops the glass getting underfoot. I've just scratched myself on this one, that's all.'

He pulled the sliver of glass from his finger, and put the empty little glass tube on the desk in front of him before sticking the finger in his mouth to suck it.

'Now, there's a nice hygienic trick!' Lucy said. 'Let me get this woman settled, and I'll put a dressing on for you—'

She was taking bottles and phials out of the drug cupboard as she spoke, inspecting the labels carefully, and her forehead creased as one bottle after the other came out.

'That's odd—'

'What is?' Barney inspected his finger, which had stopped bleeding—not that he intended to say so. Letting Lucy put a dressing on it would be most agreeable.

'Insulin. Plain insulin. I had a huge stock of it, I know I did, because I had to order a lot for a patient who was going home. Only she had a sudden heart attack and died, and I didn't have to use it for her. That's *odd*.'

Barney raised his hand, and looked at her, his finger forgotten, and then turned his head as a trolley went clattering past the open office door. Almost without thinking, he got up, and moved swiftly over to it, to stop the porter who was pushing it and stared down at the woman on it.

She was deeply unconscious, and her face was dry and wrinkled, and she was breathing heavily, with deep sighing breaths.

'Oh, my God,' Barney said softly, and stood back to let the trolley move on.

'What's the matter?' Lucy said curiously, and then turned to Nurse Crowther, who was following the trolley into the ward, a set of case notes under her arm.

'Nurse Crowther—look, nip across to Male Medical and get a hundred units of plain insulin from them, will you? I can't think what's happened to ours, unless the night staff *lent* it to someone and didn't tell me. I know we haven't used it. Then go and help Dr Hickson give it and set up the drip, as soon as he gets here—'

Nurse Crowther nodded and went away, passing John Hickson at the door. He looked a little more like himself now, and he nodded briefly at Barney and Lucy as he took the notes from the hands of Nurse Crowther.

'I'll put up a drip, Sister,' he said, and Lucy nodded crisply.

'I think you'll find everything ready, Dr Hickson. Nurse will be back with the insulin in a moment—' and with a brief smile at Barney, Lucy led the way down the ward and she and Hickson disappeared behind the screens round bed seventeen.

When she came back, Barney had gone, and she felt a curious sense of resentment. He might have said he was going, she thought miserably. After being with her all morning, he might have *said*—

The new patient claimed her attention then, and for the next few hours she was too busy to think much about Barney or anything but the comatose woman's condition. But at half past six, when the woman had at last shown signs of recovering somewhat, and Lucy was supervising the serving of the patients' suppers, he came back.

She turned from the shiny metal trolley, a plate and a serving spoon in her hands and looked at him, and he looked back at her with his face white and bleak.

And just as she had that time before—was it

only yesterday? It felt like an eternity ago—she turned the job in hand over to Nurse Crowther, and led him into her office, and sat him down, and perched in the desk beside him.

'What's happened?' she asked, keeping her voice as matter-of-fact as possible. 'Don't look like that, Barney. Tell me what's happened.'

'I murdered him.'

She stared at him, feeling the colour drain out of her cheeks. 'What did you say?'

He looked at her, and managed a strained smile.

'Oh, my God, not deliberately! But I murdered him. He was a fit man, and I killed him—'

He began to shake, first his hands, and then his neck and shoulders until his whole body was trembling, and Lucy slid to her feet, and pulled him up, and put her arms round him and held him close, straining him against her own warm strong body, and gradually the shaking stopped, and he lifted his head from her neck where he had buried it, and looked down at her.

'I know how it was done,' he said. 'I know how it was done. And whoever wanted to do it used me—*me*—to do it for him. I—think I'm going to be sick—'

And he was, and she held his head as he leaned over the wash-hand basin in the corner of the office, and mopped his sweating brow and made him sit down again, shaken and spent.

'All right,' she said crisply. 'All right. You now know what you suspected was true *is* true. All right. But you don't have to panic. Just take it easy, and tell me exactly what you've discovered.'

He took a deep shuddering breath, and then looked up at her ruefully.

'Sorry. I do get into a flap. But it was—such a shock to know I had actually killed a man, even though it was in all innocence. Listen.'

His eyes seemed to glaze slightly, as though he was watching some invisible action.

'The private theatre anaesthetic room is very nicely organised. There's a rack on the drug side, with holes cut in it. And in each hole there's an ampoule of the drugs needed for an anaesthetic. One of pentothal. One of sterile water to mix it with. One of adrenalin, one of curare—you know. And when I work there, I automatically use the ampoules prepared.

'Yesterday morning I did that. I picked up the sterile water ampoule, and opened it and drew the water out and put it into the pentothal. Then I dropped the empty ampoule in my pocket the way I always do. And I gave the mixture to that poor bloody sailor. Only it hadn't been mixed with water. It had been mixed with insulin. Three hundred units of insulin. Enough to kill an ox!'

His voice rose again, and Lucy put out her hand and touched his cheek, and he held her hand against it with his own, and took a deep breath.

'It was your insulin, Lucy. From this ward. It must have been. I've been over to the Pharmacy, and I've checked. Of course they're in a fearful state there, trying to sort out what's what after the fire, but the main drug supplies weren't damaged, and Bruce swears no insulin was missing from his stock. And I've checked on the other wards, and they haven't missed any. Only *you* have. And there's another thing. The sterile water ampoules. The Pharmacy prepares them. They aren't brought in, ready filled and sealed. They do their own. Someone stole your supply of plain insulin, and put it in an ampoule labelled sterile water, and set it in the private theatre waiting for me to use it. And I did.'

Lucy wrinkled her forehead, and rubbed her face as she tried to think clearly.

'But I don't understand—*why*? Just putting an ampoule of insulin in the theatre—that's crazy. *Anyone* might have used it.'

He shook his head. 'No,' he said drearily. 'Whoever put it there knew what he was doing. The operating lists go up in advance, the night before. The murderer just had to put it there, and leave it to me to do his killing for him. It must have been Quayle he was after—and got later on with the blood. But the emergency was put in instead and he got it, poor devil—'

They sat and stared at each other, and then

Barney said huskily, 'What do I do now? I *know* that's what happened. Now the symptoms the man showed make sense. The sweating—a classic sign of insulin coma. The way he was breathing. The way his blood pressure reacted. It all makes *sense* now. But how the hell am I going to prove it? Prove it wasn't with my knowledge, I mean, that I gave the stuff?'

'I don't know,' Lucy said. 'But it doesn't matter, does it? You don't *have* to prove it. It's enough you've found how that man died. It's not your problem to find out the way or the who. Come on—'

She went to the door, and Barney put out a hand to stop her.

'Come on? Where?'

'To see Spain, of course. Where else? Come on, Barney. You'll have to face him sooner or later, so come now. It'll be easier this way. We've got to take a chance on his believing you.'

CHAPTER NINE

Spain sat with his chin sunk into his heavy neck staring unwinkingly at Barney as he tried to explain as lucidly as he could what had happened the previous morning in the private theatres anaesthetic room. Once or twice Lucy cut in with a word of explanation, and then his eyes shifted to her face, but otherwise he made no move at all.

But when Barney stopped speaking, he raised his chin, and said a little petulantly, 'It sounds very plausible—like mystery films and plays are plausible. But is it *likely*? I mean—untraceable poisons an' all that jazz! That's what it seems like to me—an' I'm a simple soul—'

'Oh, for God's sake man!' Barney was suddenly flamingly angry. 'D'you think I'm making it up? I've spent the whole afternoon chasing around the hospital checking on this, and I tell you that's what happened! Why in hell's name should I come here with a—a trumped up story out of a mystery film, as you put it? There'd be no sense in that—'

'Oh, yes, there would,' Spain said mildly. 'If it was your negligence killed the man. That'd be a very good reason.'

Lucy put out a hand to restrain Barney, who looked almost murderous with rage, and spoke quickly.

'You like facts, Inspector Spain. You've said that often enough. And we've brought you some. My insulin stock has disappeared. Barney has the empty ampoule it was in—'

'Ah, yes.' Spain reached out a long arm for the little glass ampoule Barney had put on the desk in front of him. 'The ampoule. Would it be possible to discover traces of insulin in this, d'you think? That would go a long way to convincing a court of law. That's all I'm interested in, y'know. Facts that can be brought to court as evidence.'

'I don't know,' Barney said sulkily. 'I'm an anaesthetist, not an analytical chemist.'

'Then we'll have to find one, won't we?' Spain put the ampoule into an envelope, and sealed it with a mobile pink tongue.

'And if he finds insulin, then I'm prepared to agree, we may have murder on our hands. Look, let's have a recap, eh? The anaesthetic room is arranged so that the drugs for the first case are set out in advance and are invariably used for that case. That's the first point. The theatre staff nurse set 'em out the night before—illegally, accordin' to that Sister Battleaxe—and then says she locked up the anaesthetic room. That's the second point. In the morning, the room was unlocked. Point three. The keys to the theatres hang in the hall where anyone can get at 'em at any time. That's point four. During the case, you needed another ampoule of water, and had to send for one, although that staff nurse said there should have been one there. Point five. That's one in favour of your theory, by the way. Obviously if some feller put the insulin ampoule in the room he wanted to make doubly sure you'd use it, so he took away the spare one.'

'Thank you!' Barney said sardonically.

'Not at all,' Spain said equably. 'Now, what

131

is point six? Yes. The man who should have been first on the list, and would have died of the insulin if it hadn't been for that poor ruddy sailor, he died later, under equally dubious circumstances. So that's another bit of circumstantial evidence in your favour.'

'Really, you get more and more obliging,' Barney snapped.

'Tut tut, Dr Elliot! You really mustn't be so touchy! What sort of a policeman would I be if I threw up my hands with joy whenever anyone came to me with what looks on the surface to be a cock and bull story, and shouted "Eureka"? A rotten policeman, that's what. Of course I've got to query it! I keep tellin' you I've got to find evidence that'll stand up in court. Now, just you calm down and stop lookin' at me as though I were Borgia's Granpa, and help me think this business out. Hold his hand or somethin', Sister Beaumont, and see if that'll soothe him a bit.'

Lucy blushed, and immediately let go of Barney's hand, which she had in fact been clutching.

'Now, let's see what we've got. A neat and tidy method of murder. Very neat, really, because from what you tell me the chances of its bein' discovered were very slim. I mean, if it had been Quayle who'd died on the table that way, would you have been all that surprised?' and he looked shrewdly at Barney.

Barney grinned a little at last. He couldn't

132

help it. 'For a non-medical type, you've got a good grasp of essentials,' he said grudgingly. 'No, I don't think I would have been. Quayle was a much older man, much less fit than that sailor. He was heavier, not in such good condition. I think I might have assumed heart failure or shock—especially as Quayle's operation would have been a much bigger one—more debilitating.'

'Which means if it hadn't been for the accident of the emergency goin' on the list first, there might have been a truly perfect murder committed—the perfect murder bein' one where no one knows murder's been done. Yes, very pretty. You've got to admire the bloke that dreamed it up, haven't you? Now, all we've got to do is find out why someone was gunnin' for Quayle, and then we've got a very good chance of findin' out who that someone was.'

He stretched suddenly. 'I've got work to do. A lot of work. Got to dig out some facts about poor departed Mr Quayle.'

'We were going to do that—' Lucy said.

'What?'

'Last night. We'd come to the same conclusion, before the fire, I mean. We were talking in the "Ship in Bottle", and though we didn't know how it was done, we were sure he had been murdered and we said then we'd go to records and find out who he was, and where he came from and everything. Only then the fire

133

happened and I forgot all about it—'

Spain smiled broadly at her. 'Well, not to fret. That's what I'm here for. Policemen never forget anything. Now, if you don't mind, I'll turn you two out of here, and get on with my job. If anything else occurs to you, come and tell me, eh? I like gettin' lots of co-operation from my suspects. It does make life so much easier. Good evenin'!'

They walked in silence back along the pathway that led from the administrative block back to the garden and thence to the courtyard and the hospital, but as they reached the garden, peaceful and pretty under the lengthening shadows of a summer evening, Barney stopped suddenly.

'I don't want to leave it to him.'

'What?'

'Spain. I don't trust that man. He's—he's as smooth as melted butter, and I don't trust him. I want to find out for myself, all about Quayle, I mean. Maybe we could find out something that would make it even more clear I didn't know about the insulin—that I didn't know I was killing that man—'

'Barney—oh, no! I'm sure he doesn't think that!' Lucy said, all her instinctive desire to protect him coming boiling to the surface.

He looked down at her upturned anxious face, and smiled a little crookedly. 'You're a sweet loyal darling, Lucy, and I could kiss you for it. But let's be realistic. That Spain thinks that I *did* kill the sailor, and won't have any compunction about trying to prove it. And he's no fool—if anyone can cook up a case on flimsy evidence, he can. I've got to protect myself.'

He touched her cheek with a gentle hand, and then turned her shoulders so that she was facing the hospital. 'You go back to the ward. I'm going to the records office to look at Quayle's notes—'

She shook her head. 'They won't be there, Barney. Will they? They'll either be still on the ward, or in the mortuary with the body, or in Stroud's office waiting for the coroner, or—almost anywhere. But they won't be in records.'

Barney swore, comprehensively. 'You're right, of course. Then I'll have to go up to the ward. Sister Palmer might know something about him—'

He started to move, walking purposefully across the grass towards the side entrance to the Private Wing, and Lucy scuttled along at his side, anxiously.

'Barney—not now! Spain'll be sure to think of the same thing and come over himself in a minute. Do you want to have him find you pumping her? Do be a little more circumspect—'

But Barney shook his head, and walked on, dodging under the low hanging branches of the copper beech, plunging them both into the heavy plum coloured shadows. Lucy pulled at his arm again, and this time managed to stop him.

'Barney, please—' she said again, and then jumped, and whirled.

'Who's that?' she said breathlessly, and then relaxed as John Hickson appeared sheepishly from the other side of the heavy gnarled trunk.

'Oh, it's you—you startled me. I do wish you wouldn't be so *silent*,' she said, and giggled a little nervously. Hickson really had alarmed her, appearing so suddenly and quietly.

'Sorry,' he said, mumbling a little. 'Better get back—' and he dodged under a particularly low branch and went loping awkwardly over the grass towards the main block.

'That bloody man—we're always falling over him,' Barney said irritably, and then took a sharp breath.

'Lucy—we *are* always falling over him, aren't we? All through this business?'

They both moved around the tree and out into the brightness on the far side, and stood staring after the figure now disappearing along the covered way and into the consultants' car park.

'I suppose we are,' she said slowly. 'Last night, at the fire—and yesterday morning in the theatres—in the anaesthetic room, in fact—'

'And then this morning it turns out he was outside Stroud's office when Bruce came over with the drug books,' Lucy finished.

'He is very involved, somehow, isn't he?' Barney said. 'D'you suppose *he*—'

'Barney, no! It couldn't be! Not Hickson. I mean, he's such a—a milk and water sort of person. And anyway, we *know* him.'

Barney looked down at her, and said soberly, 'But haven't you realised that already, Lucy? Whoever the murderer is, it's someone we know, someone we've worked with, someone who's a friend, maybe. It could even be me, according to Spain.'

She looked up at him, gravely, and shook her head. 'It isn't you. It couldn't be—'

'But why couldn't it be? I had the same opportunity everyone else had. Maybe the same motive—whatever that is, because we don't know yet. Why couldn't it be me?'

'Because I—because I like you too much,' she said simply, and felt the infuriating childish blush redden her round cheeks again. She had so nearly said 'because I love you—' But that would never do. Not now. Not yet.

He grinned. 'That convinces *me*, but it wouldn't convince Spain. You'll have to do better than that.'

'I *could* convince Spain!' she said after a moment. 'Of course I could! Listen, Barney— it's agreed that the first man—the sailor—died by accident. I mean, he wasn't an intended victim?'

'Agreed.'

'Well, then!' Lucy cried triumphantly. 'You *knew* he was on the list, didn't you? If you'd intended to kill Quayle, you'd have saved that insulin ampoule for him, wouldn't you? You wouldn't have gone ahead and got rid of that sailor only to have to deal with Quayle later. And you wouldn't have insisted the sailor's death was unusual the way you did. It couldn't be you! I'm going right back to Spain to tell him so—'

He seized her arm, and hugged it to his side. 'Bless you. But that can wait. Right now, what Spain wants is facts, not the convictions of someone who—likes me. If that's the word you really meant.'

'It'll do for the present,' she said, a little awkwardly, and hurried on. 'But I suppose you're right. What are we going to do then? I still think we shouldn't go talking to Sister Palmer now, because it's odds on Spain will be after her. Look, let's have some supper, hmm? I'm due off duty in fifteen minutes anyway. I'll go to the ward and hand over properly to Nurse Crowther—'

'And then we'll go over to Chalky and get a sandwich and a drink,' Barney said. 'You're on. We'll have a go at Sister Palmer later on, before she goes off for the evening. What time will that be?'

'She had a morning off, so she'll be there till half past eight or so,' Lucy said. 'I'll see you over the road in half an hour, then. I want to change into mufti.'

They had an agreeable supper, by tacit consent not discussing the case at all. They talked about themselves, about their respective families, their likes and dislikes, and for Lucy, certainly, it was an hour in which she found herself slipping more and more deeply into an emotional whirlwind. The physical attraction Barney had for her was cemented by the many things they had in common. But at eight o'clock, she forced herself to emerge from the happy daze in which she had been wallowing, forced herself to remember that right now there was more to life than the furthering of what promised to be a more than agreeable relationship.

'If we're going to talk to Sister Palmer about Quayle, we'd better go over to the Wing now,' she said, and stood up to brush the crumbs of sausage rolls and potato crisps from her lap.

'I suppose so—' Barney said reluctantly, and stood up too.

'Oh—look. There's Jeff. Hi, feller. Any news?'

Jeff hooked a finger at Chalky behind the bar, who nodded, and began to draw his usual pint of half-and-half.

'What can be news?' he said, dropping on to the bench beside them to sit sprawling. 'I've had dozens of nosy policemen prowling around the department all day, asking stupid questions about crossmatching and keys. All they've decided is that anyone could have got into the lab at any time, that anyone could have meddled with a bottle of blood from the fridge—all of which I'd told 'em anyway. The only difference between their point of view and mine is that they aren't convinced someone meddled—while I keep telling 'em someone did, because I certainly crossmatched the right blood. Ah, what the hell. I'm fed up with the whole business. Have a drink with me. I need company.'

'We can't,' Barney said. 'We're going to talk to Sister Palmer in the wing—trying to find out more about Quayle, you see, and we think perhaps she'll know, as the Sister in charge of the ward he was in. I'd like to, really, but—'

'I'll phone over if you like,' Lucy said, touched by Jeff's miserable face. 'Have a drink with Jeff, Barney, and I'll get Palmer to come over here. I daresay I can persuade her—'

Barney smiled at her. 'Nice Lucy,' he murmured. 'OK, Jeff. Same as yours, then,' and Lucy went across the bar to duck under the counter and use the phone in Chalky's snug but incredibly untidy office.

When she came back her face was pink with suppressed excitement.

'Barney!' she said. 'Listen, we're in luck. Palmer says there's a woman there—says she's a friend of Quayle's, and she's come to collect his effects. If we go over right now, we could talk to her—'

140

'What!' Barney jumped to his feet. 'My God, that *is* useful. Coming Jeff? You're as involved as I am—'

But Jeff shook his head morosely. 'Hell, no. I've had enough for one day. I'm content to leave the poking and prying to that bloody policeman. If he wants to think I'm a murderer, let him prove it—' and he buried his face in his tankard.

'I'm not so trusting,' Barney said dryly. 'This woman'll be worth talking to, whoever she is. And if we can get at her before Spain does, we may get something useful. Come on, man.'

But Jeff shook his head again, and Barney shrugged, and taking Lucy by the elbow steered her out of the now crowded saloon bar.

They crossed the main hall of the Private Wing, which was busy with departing visitors, and went up in the lift to the second floor in silence. Lucy felt obscurely that the answer to the whole mystery was waiting for them up there. Surely this woman, this friend of Quayle's, must have been close to him? Only the person designated on the admission form by the patient as his next of kin could be given a patient's effects, so surely she could help them? Surely she could give them some insight into the man, an insight that would show why someone had been so anxious to get rid of him?

Colin Jackson and Harry Caspar were waiting by the lift as they reached the second floor, and Jackson pulled the gates back irritably.

'If you have no work to do, I have,' he snapped at Barney as he and Lucy stepped out. 'What are you doing over here, anyway, keeping the lifts busy for no reason?'

'There's a relative of Quayle's I want to talk to,' Barney said, equally sharply. 'Do you mind?'

Jackson shrugged. 'None of my concern, I suppose. Bad enough the police are everywhere, I should have thought, without you opting in. All I ask is you do nothing to hold up the work of the hospital, even if you can't do anything to further it,' and he slammed the gates shut, and stabbed a button, so that he and an embarrassed looking Harry were carried upwards.

'Bad tempered louse,' Barney muttered, staring after them, but Lucy touched his elbow soothingly.

'Forget him, Barney. Come and talk to this woman. I'm sure she'll be able to tell us something useful—'

But when they walked into Sister Palmer's office, her heart fell. The woman who was standing there looked so forbiddingly at them that she knew at once that she wouldn't want to answer any questions.

She was a big woman, with aggressively blonde hair piled on top of her head in a highly fashionable style that was at least ten years too young for her, for she looked about forty-five, in spite of her careful make-up and well-corseted body under the expensive well-cut clothes. She was holding a large black brief case as well as a very rich looking black crocodile bag, which matched her spindly heeled shoes, and she stood with her feet planted well apart as she stared at them.

'Well?' she said, and her voice was harsh. 'Sister says you want to talk to me. Who are you, and what do you want?'

'I'm Dr Elliot,' Barney said. 'And this is Sister Beaumont. Look, I'm sorry to—to bother you at a time like this. I mean, I know how it is when one has been bereaved, and I'm truly sorry—'

'Well? Get to the point,' she said. 'And leave my feelings out of it. They're none of your damned business.'

Barney blinked, and then nodded. 'All right,' he said crisply. 'Briefly, the death of Mr Quayle has—puzzled us. There are aspects that need investigating—'

'So I've heard. The police are here.'

Barney nodded. 'Precisely. And what I want to know is—'

'Are you police?'

'I told you—I'm a doctor—Mrs—er—Miss—er—'

She ignored his groping for her name and went on as though he hadn't spoken.

'Because unless you're police you have no right to question me. I've told Sister Whatsit here where I can be reached by the police, and if they want to come talking to me, that's their business and mine. It certainly isn't yours.'

'I realise that I have no official standing as a questioner,' Barney said as patiently as he could. 'But I can assure you I—we—are as anxious as they are to clear this matter up. More anxious, in some ways. And I'd be more than grateful if you'd just tell us one or two things about Mr Quayle that might—'

'No,' she said baldly. 'You can stuff your gratitude. I talk to no one unless I must.' And she pushed past them to the door.

Barney reached out and took her arm, and she stopped and looked down at his hand with such an expression of cold disdain on her face that he let go.

'I told you,' she said harshly. 'Are you too stupid to take it in? I'm not talking to anyone unless I've got to, so you can go to hell—' and she walked out, slamming the door behind her, leaving the three of them in a stupified silence. They heard the rattle of the lift gates and the whine of the motor diminishing before they moved.

'Well, I'll be damned,' Barney said softly. 'I'll be double damned.'

'People do behave like that when they're upset, sometimes,' Lucy said. 'I mean, it's a shock when people die, people you care for—'

'That one?' Sister Palmer almost snorted. 'That one, upset? Don't you believe it, my dear.

144

She's as hard as bloody nails, I tell you. When she came up, I took one look at her and I knew. When she marched in here, I said to myself, there's angry! And she was! Not that she said much, mind you. She just said she was Mr Quayle's next of kin, and showed me her copy of the admission form, and said she wanted his things. So what could I do? I tried to say I was sorry he was dead, but she just bit my head off. And all she wanted was his brief case. Wouldn't take his clothes or anything else, not even his watch, which was a good one. Told me to throw them away! I had a right job to keep her here to talk to you, I promise, though I knew it wouldn't be much good—'

'Only wanted his brief case?' Barney spoke sharply. 'Then that's the important thing. I mean, there must be something in it that offers an answer to all this, and she knew it. She *must* know something if he gave her as his next of kin! Look, I'm not letting her get away with this—'

He made for the door, and then stopped. 'Oh, hell, what's the use? Even if I caught up with her, what could I do? I couldn't take the case from her by brute force. Not that that'd work, anyway. She's a damned sight tougher than I am, to look at her—'

'Tell Spain,' Lucy said.

'Eh?'

'Oh, do let's have some sense, Barney! I can see you want to do as much as you can to sort

145

this out by yourself, but it *is* Spain's job, and there's no sense in trying to do things on our own if we make a mess of it! Tell Spain about her, and about the brief case, and he'll talk to her. He'll get it out of her, because he's police and he's got the authority, and anyway, he'd get anything out of anybody, even a formidable female like that Mrs—what's her name, Palmer?'

Sister Palmer leafed through some papers on her desk.

'Miss Roberta Vickers,' she said at length. 'Lives on a houseboat in that Yacht Basin west of Northwestern Dock. The *Bobby Vee*, it's called.'

'On a boat? Then she must be stinking with money. It costs a bomb to live that way,' Barney said. 'Oh, hell, Lucy, I suppose you're right. Look, we'll go and find Spain. He may still be over in the Admin block. Thanks, Sister Palmer, for trying to help. We'll let you know what happens.'

'Do. I'm that curious,' Sister Palmer said, and grinned a little wickedly at Lucy. 'If you've time to think of more than one Sister at a time, that is.'

They used the stairs, because the lift was busy with visitors, and as Lucy scuttled down the broad polished treads behind Barney her spirits, which had taken a sharp dive at the response they had got from Miss Vickers, began to rise again. Spain, she felt obscurely,

146

would know how to get the facts out of her. She wouldn't have said as much to Barney, not for the world, for she knew he disliked the Inspector, but she found Spain an oddly comforting personality, despite his air of flippancy.

They emerged into the garden through the side door, a garden now dark and sighing a little in the night breeze. Lucy shrank a little closer to Barney as they hurried across the grass towards the path that led to the Admin block. She wished, not for the first time, that the garden was better lit. It was odd how eerie it could seem on a moonless night.

And then, suddenly, Barney tripped and went sprawling, just as they passed the big bed of roses that starred one side of the lawn. Lucy could smell the sudden sweetness of crushed flowers as she bent to help him to his feet.

'What the hell?' Barney said, rubbing tenderly at his knees. 'Someone's left a rake there or something—'

He bent then, and felt about in the darkness, and then stood up so sharply that Lucy, standing close behind him, nearly went sprawling in her turn.

'Just a minute—' he said, and fumbled in his pocket. Then, there was the scrape of a match, and a small light sprang up, flickered and then settled to burn fairly steadily in Barney's cupped palm.

She saw then, as she looked down. There,

sprawled on the grass, her feet with the expensive crocodile shoes bent awkwardly under her, and her face turned upwards with blind open eyes staring up with a sort of ferocious surprise, was Roberta Vickers.

And it didn't take her nursing experience to tell Lucy the woman was dead. The pool of blood which was still spreading thickly and stickily across her chest showed that all too clearly.

CHAPTER TEN

'Oh, my God,' Barney said very softly, and then the match went out, plunging them into darkness again, and Lucy felt horror rise in her like a tide.

Beside her, she felt Barney fumble once more for matches, and then there was the comforting flicker of light again, and her fear receded a little, leaving her shaking but in control of herself.

'Here—' she said, and her voice sounded husky in her own ears. 'I've got a lighter—' and she fished it out of the pocket of her jacket.

In the steadier light it gave, they could see more clearly. The woman was lying on her back, her legs twisted awkwardly, and beside her her crocodile bag lay open, with its contents sprawling on the grass—make-up,

148

little gilt tubes of lipstick and eyeshadow glittering in the light of their tiny flame, a black morocco purse, a handkerchief, a small red-covered notebook, a pencil with tassel on it, a blue tassel. Lucy took in the details greedily, anything to stop herself from looking at that blank horribly grimacing face and the blood-soaked coat beneath it.

She had seen death many times, but never violent death, like this, death deliberately inflicted. She realised with sudden intense clarity just why Barney had been sick when he knew for certain that he had been the instrument that actually caused the death of the sailor.

'Lucy—are you all right?' Barney's voice brought her back, made her realise that she had been swaying a little, and she swallowed and said as evenly as she could, 'I'm fine—just fine—'

'I've got to get Spain,' Barney said. 'I must get him—' All his distrust of the Inspector somehow evaporated in the face of this newest development. 'If I only knew exactly where he *was*—'

'Phone from the wing, Barney,' Lucy said, and felt her jaw shake as she spoke. 'Switchboard'll put out a call for him—say it's urgent—go on, Barney. Now—'

'But—he might—I mean, whoever did this. He might still be about. He must be—' Barney reached out his hand and touched the dead

149

face. 'She hasn't been dead more than a few moments. I ought to look for him.'

'Are you mad?' In the face of such foolhardiness, Lucy's fear seemed to melt away. 'Go and get Spain. I'll stay here and watch—her. You phone and come straight back—'

'You'll be all right?'

'Of course I will.' All her native common sense was coming back, as the initial shock of their discovery receded. 'Whoever did this is heading away from here as fast as he can, you can be sure of that. The sooner you get Spain the better—do *hurry*, Barney—' and she gave him a little push.

'Right. If anything worries you, shriek blue—shriek as loudly as you can,' he said, and then he turned and she heard his footsteps thudding away over the black grass.

And then there was silence again, as she heard the distant door of the wing slam behind him, and she stood in the dark garden with only a dead body for company, and a cigarette lighter between herself and complete blackness.

The lighter spluttered a little, and the flame sank, and quickly she extinguished it, and turned the little silver square upside down and shook it, to send the fuel back into the wick, and relit it with a quick flick of the spring.

And as the light flared up again, illuminating the circle which held just herself and the body at her feet, she saw it. The little red-covered notebook moved in the sudden sharp light, and then was gone.

She hadn't really seen the hand that removed it, but she knew that it had emerged from the bank of rose bushes and picked up that notebook. And without thinking, she hurled herself at the ground, at the edge of the flower bed, trying to see who it was that lay there screened by the leafy low bushes and the heavy-headed drooping roses.

And as she did, the lighter went spinning from her hand, leaving her in thick darkness, and something happened at the back of her head, something hot and hard and cold and soft all at once, something that made her feel sick, and made someone somewhere scream and scream in a high pitched note that made her feel ill. And even as she felt the blackness get inside her head and her mouth, choking her, she knew the screams were her own, and that something across her mouth was trying to prevent them from coming out.

She was swimming, pushing up from the bottom of the blue-green pool, towards the sunlight above, and it was a very special pool because she could breathe under the water. She could hear, too, with a clarity that was surprising. 'It's Barney,' she thought, 'Barney calling me. I'd better get out—' And then her head broke the surface and she opened her eyes and the sun was the central light fitting in the

151

Casualty waiting room, and not the sun at all, and she felt faintly aggrieved, and wanted to tell Barney how unfair it was.

She turned her head to look for him, and the sudden sharp pain in the back of her head made her whimper, and then he was there. His hand was on hers, and he was leaning over and looking at her with his grey eyes wide and anxious, and his face carved into a heavy frown of worry.

But as she looked up at him, the frown went away, and he smiled with intense relief and said, 'That's better—'

Someone moved the room then. Barney was still beside her, but the ceiling was moving, and she realised she was lying on a trolley, and someone was pushing it.

'What's—what's happening?' Her voice seemed very thick.

'You're a bit concussed, love,' Barney said. 'Don't fret you—you'll be fine soon. But right now we're taking you to sick bay for the night. You've got an abrasion on your scalp at the back, but there's nothing much to it, and you'll be fine in the morning—fine in this morning—'

His voice disappeared in a series of repetitions of the phrase, echoing and diminishing in the long corridors of her mind, and the next time she opened her eyes they were lifting her into a cool bed, and Barney had gone. She said his name, once, sleepily and someone said, 'In the morning—' and she

152

closed her eyes again, feeling good suddenly. Barney, in the morning, and he'd said she'd feel fine then, so of course she would, not sick and pain-filled like now.

She woke with a beastly headache that throbbed behind her eyes and in her neck and made her feel sick, and she was grateful for the wash the night staff nurse gave her, grateful for the dose of aspirin that relieved much of her headache. By the time Barney arrived she had breakfasted on a little lemon tea and dry toast and felt weak and rather floppy, but reasonably in command of herself.

He put his head round the door, and his face lit up when she smiled at him.

'Lucy, you look about fifteen, in that white nightshirt. How are you, love? Rotten?'

'A bit on the fragile side,' Lucy admitted. 'And I'm sorry about the nightshirt. It's a theatre gown—no one this morning had time to go and get me my own things. Barney, what happened?'

He came and perched on the side of the bed, and picked up one of her hands to hold it cradled in both of his.

'I was the biggest bloody fool out last night,' he said soberly. 'I can't tell you how sorry I am, Lucy. When I heard you screaming like that, I thought—I don't know what I thought. I think I died a little. I hadn't even got as far as the wing porter's lodge phone, and I heard you scream and went running back as though all

153

the hounds of hell were after me.'

'But what *happened*?' Lucy said again.

'I got there the same time as Spain and Travers. They'd been in the Admin Block, and they heard you too, and came running. I got you back to Casualty and they dealt with the body—'

The body. At last she remembered. All morning, ever since she had woken, she had been trying to remember, but she hadn't been able to take recollection beyond the point at which she and Barney had been walking across the grass towards the Admin Block, looking for Spain. But now she remembered, and she turned her head, painfully, and said urgently, 'The notebook—'

'What? What notebook?'

'The one in her bag—I mean, it had fallen out with the other things, and it was lying on the grass, and then the lighter went out, and I shook it to get more light and put it on again and I saw the hand take it away, and then—'

'Calm down, love, calm down—' Barney pushed her gently back against her pillows and stroked her forehead gently. 'Don't get so excited—' And Lucy realised she had been gabbling, and subsided.

'Now, tell me quietly. Just take your time and tell me quietly. What about this notebook?'

Behind him the door clicked and opened, and the disapproving face of Sister in charge of

154

the Staff Sick Bay appeared, with Inspector Spain and Sergeant Travers close behind her.

'Sister, are you willing to talk to these people? Because if you are not I'm quite prepared to refuse them admission to this room. And if you think being nagged by policemen is too much for her, Dr Elliot, then I shall be equally firm—'

Barney looked at Lucy consideringly, and she smiled, a little shakily, and said, 'I'd really better talk to them, Ingram. I've got things to explain, and they ought to know—'

'I'll throw them out when she's had enough, Sister, I promise,' Barney said, and Sister Ingram sniffed and nodded, and went away leaving Travers and Spain standing at the foot of Lucy's bed.

'A right old mother hen, isn't she?' Spain said conversationally. 'Does she always flap around like that?'

'She's a very good nurse, and looks after the sick staff very well,' Lucy said loyally. 'If I were in charge of me, I wouldn't let you talk to me either. I've been concussed.' She couldn't help grinning a little then. She sounded exactly like a child boasting about a minor illness, and Spain grinned back in a companionable fashion, and came and sat on the other side of her bed with his hands crossed on his knees, and a benevolent look on his face as he looked down at her.

'Well, well, well. A right little warrior, aren't

155

you? Gettin' biffed on the head in that fashion. Not clever, Sister, not clever at all—'

'It was my fault,' Barney said. 'I should never have left her. But I was so sure the murderer must have gone away from the body, that there'd be more likelihood of danger to the person who went to phone, that I left her and went myself, and I could kick myself for it—'

'Yes, well, we all know about the way love's young dream makes a feller feel. Blame yourself for everything, even the bee that stings her. But if we waste time listening to all that, that old hen out there'll be in with a broom to chase us out. So let's get down to some facts. Sister, can you tell me what happened last night?'

'I think so,' Lucy said. 'Where do I start?'

'Why were you walkin' across the garden in the pitch dark? Or is that a silly question?' And Spain looked slyly at Barney who frowned irritably.

'We were looking for you—' Lucy plunged into an account of the evening, the way they had decided to seek information about Quayle, and had contacted Sister Palmer, about meeting Roberta Vickers, the whole story. He listened carefully, and when she had finished telling him about the disappearing notebook sighed heavily and shook his head.

'I was slow off the mark there, wasn't I, Travers? Yes. Should have gone to see Sister Palmer myself, and got some information

156

about this Vickers woman. I'll tell you the truth, Dr Elliot, Sister Beaumont. I wasn't what you might call convinced about the murder of that there sailor, or even the murder of Quayle. Y'see, I haven't that much faith in hospitals. I'm not a bit surprised when people die in 'em, or when doctors make mistakes—'

'But we didn't!' Barney burst in.

'I know you didn't—now,' Spain said soothingly. 'But yesterday, I wasn't so certain. But I've had that ampoule looked at by the analytical people, and we've done some prowlin' round in that laboratory, and I'll tell you somethin'—there *was* insulin in that there ampoule, and we found some labels for blood bottles in the lab. And there ain't supposed to be any such labels lyin' around, accordin' to Dr Heath. We found these labels hidden right at the back of a store cupboard, and what with that and the insulin in the ampoule, and now that woman gettin' killed, and you gettin' biffed—well, there's not much doubt now, is there? No. We've got a right juicy case here. Arson, drug runnin' and now old fashioned murder—done in a very far fetched fashion, but murder all the same. If I'd'a realised yesterday evenin' about all this, well, I'd'a been investigatin' Quayle like a mad thing. I'd have talked to Sister Palmer about him, and copped a look at that Vickers woman—maybe even have got that notebook out of her. As it is—' he shook his head mournfully. 'As it is, I've got to be honest and admit I've made a right muck up of this. We've had another murder, and lost a valuable source of information. I feel rotten—' And he looked so miserable that instinctively Lucy put out a hand and patted his arm.

But he grinned at her, and said, 'Take no notice of me, m'dear. We all make mistakes— even policemen—and I'm not going to let it get me down. Now, the next thing I've got to do is go and have a good look at the stuff they found on the Vickers woman—her handbag and that—'

'What about the brief case?' Lucy asked.

'No brief case there when we got there. I reckon that's why the murderer hung about. To get his hands on it, and on that notebook. My, but I'd give a lot to know what was in that notebook, wouldn't you, Travers? Yes. Ah, well, not to fret.

'We'll have a look over that houseboat— what was it called? The *Bobby Vee*? yes. We'll have a good look at that, and maybe that'll tell us something about the mysterious Mr Quayle. There's more to that feller than we know, that's for sure. Well, Sister Beaumont! You look as though you need a bit of a kip. Right peaky lookin' you are. Travers and me, we'll go off and do some work, and leave you and your boy friend to it. But if you'll take my advice, Dr Elliot—' and he looked sternly at Barney, 'you'll not hang around too long. She's concussed, you know, and she needs time to recover.'

And he nodded affably and went away with Sergeant Travers, leaving Barney furious and Lucy laughing weakly.

For the next twenty-four hours Lucy remained in Sick Bay, rapidly recovering her normal good spirits, and enjoying holding court in a mild way. Several of the hospital staff came to visit her, Derek Foster and Harry Caspar coming over after supper in the evening, followed by Jeff Heath and Sister Palmer. This latter visitor curled up at the foot of Lucy's bed and settled down to enjoy herself enormously. There was nothing Sister Palmer liked better than to spend time in male medical company.

Barney, of course, visited too, and sat beside Lucy holding her hand and apparently not caring who saw him do it. This warmed her greatly, though she couldn't be quite sure whether it was the pressure of his hand on hers that made her feel so good, or the publicity of the action. A little of each, probably. Anyway, she felt remarkably happy, sitting there in bed with the ghost of a headache and a sticky plaster on her scalp.

It was inevitable that they should talk about the murders. It was Sister Palmer who started them off by asking flatly, 'Well? What's been happening? Anyone got hold of anything now? We've been talking our heads off in the Sisters' dining room but it's a waste of time because nobody knows a thing! One of you must know *something*—'

'Do you know about the way the first man was killed?' Derek Foster said, with relish. 'Insulin, that's what—I got that from Spain—' and he recounted accurately what Barney had discovered, with Barney himself nodding agreement.

'And I'll tell you something else,' Derek went on. 'He's been checking on alibis, Spain, I mean, and he's worked out exactly when the switch was made—when the insulin filled ampoule was planted. The staff nurse on nights on the third floor of the wing complained of feeling a draught at around quarter past four— she swears the theatre doors were opened, because that's the only place the draught could have come from—anyway, Spain reckoned that was the moment when it was done, so he's been checking on everyone. And I'm the only one of the medical staff with a real alibi!'

'How's that?' Caspar asked.

'Because the night staff called me to Casualty at quarter to five, to see the sailor,' Derek said triumphantly. 'Spain has paced it all out, and he's convinced I couldn't have got to the theatres and back to my room in time for the night nurse to call me. Oh, yes, and Sir James is OK too. I phoned him at home, remember, and he lives a good fifteen miles away, so he'd never have had time either. But the rest of you—well, anyone of you could

160

have done it.'

There was a silence, and then Lucy said miserably, 'It's hateful to think of someone you know, someone you work with, being a murderer. Couldn't it be an outsider of some sort?'

'No, ducky, it couldn't,' Derek said cheerfully. 'You heard Bruce. Only someone who really knows the ins and outs of this place—and it's a complicated sort of a joint—could have cooked these drug books. And anyway, whoever did all this knows the hospital geography inside out. It's obviously one of us—a doctor or a senior nurse—and I'm bloody glad I've been cleared, I can promise you.'

'But *who*? Who could possibly—' Lucy began, and then Derek cut in again.

'You could work it out, you know. Eliminate people.'

'How do you mean?' Barney looked interested.

'Well,' Derek settled himself more comfortably on the window sill on which he was sitting and lit a cigarette. 'Work it out this way. Whoever planted the insulin didn't know that the list had been changed, right? If he had, he'd have made sure the wrong bloke didn't get it. Well, I knew, and you knew, so that's us eliminated—though I was anyway—oh, and old Sir James is eliminated too. Nurse Cooper knew—the staff nurse in theatres—so she's

161

out. So did Sister Palmer, so *she's* out. She knew because Quayle was her patient. Right, who does that leave on Spain's list of suspects? Sister Osgood, and Colin Jackson, Jeff and Harry, and—who else? Oh, yes, John Hickson—'

'John Hickson—' Barney said sharply, and they turned and stared at him.

'He—hell, I hate to say this, but I've already noticed the way he keeps bobbing up. Everywhere you turn in this case, there's John Hickson hanging around with a face like a parboiled fish—'

'Unkind—' murmured Lucy.

'Well, I'm sorry, but it's true. Why *does* he hang around so?'

'Oh, I can tell you *that*,' Sister Palmer said. 'If it's hanging around the Nurses' Home you mean.'

'The Nurses' Home? I hadn't really meant—Yes—I suppose you're right. He was there the night of the fire, in the garden, and again yesterday—'

'Well, of course he was!' Palmer said. 'Poor silly fool's in love. He spends hours standing around and hiding, by the tree, or on the path through to Admin., just staring at Nurse Cooper's window. It's the silliest thing you ever saw, and all the nurses are laughing at him, even Cooper. And the poor sap thinks no one knows. Between ourselves, I think he might even have a streak of the Peeping Tom

162

about him—'

'Ah, come off it, Palmer!' Derek Foster said, and laughed. 'I can well believe he'd go mooning around under a girl's window doing nothing practical about climbing inside, the way any real man would, but Peeping Tom? Never in a million years!'

Palmer shrugged, and Barney said, almost with relief, 'Well, that clears up that point, I suppose. I'm glad. I don't really enjoy suspecting people.'

'It could be a cover-up,' Jeff said. 'Quite a good one, really.'

'I suppose so,' Barney said, and then shook his head a little irritably. 'Oh, for God's sake, let's stop talking about it! I've heard nothing but mutterings about this wretched business for—it feels like a lifetime. And anyway, Lucy's had enough flap and chatter. Go away, all of you. Go on, scram.'

They wished her well, and went away, and when they were alone, Barney pulled his chair closer to the head of Lucy's bed, and propped his chin on his hands, so that his face was very close to hers.

'Have you forgiven me, Lucy?'

'What on earth for, Barney? What have you done?'

'Left you alone with a murderer.'

'Oh, for pity's sake, be quiet about that! You weren't to know! It all happened so quickly, anyway. Finding her, and deciding what to do—if we'd thought, there was no reason for me to stay behind anyway. I should have come with you to phone. But it was so instinctive—to stay with the body, I mean. One always does stay with patients, and somehow I looked on her as a patient.'

'I rather think I did. Maybe that's why I left you so willingly.'

'Either way, forget it. It's not important.' Lucy smiled at him then, letting all her feeling for him show in her face. 'But it's nice of you to care.'

'Nice?' He smiled back, his own face as expressive. 'That's one hell of a word—' And he leaned forwards, and kissed her gently, and then rather more firmly.

And for Lucy the next hour was one of quite remarkable happiness. As she said to Barney when she kissed him goodnight, at last, 'It seems all wrong—to be so happy, in the middle of murder. But I can't help it. I am happy.'

'And you'll be happier yet. Goodnight, my love.' And he left her to sleep deeply and contentedly through the remnants of her concussion.

CHAPTER ELEVEN

Lucy was given a week's sick leave in which to recuperate. after being discharged from Sick

Bay, and since Barney was still not permitted to work alone, pending the inquest on the sailor (which was delayed while the police continued their enquiries) they were able to spend a very agreeable time. The weather was warm, and they swam at the local pool several times, and dined and went to theatres, and altogether behaved more like a pair of starry eyed lovers than suspects in a most unpleasant triple murder case—murders complicated by drug-running and arson.

But they felt no guilt about their gaiety because somehow the whole investigation seemed to have ground to a halt. Spain mooched about the hospital, with Travers close behind him, looking more and more lugubrious. By the end of the week he wasn't even able to raise a smile, let alone one of his flip remarks. He did tell Barney, when they met in the hospital coffee shop three days after the murder of Roberta Vickers, that the visit to the *Bobby Vee* had told him nothing.

'The ruddy ship had been stripped to the woodwork. Not a piece of paper, not so much as a bag with the name of a shop on it could I find. No letters. Nothin'. Even the phone book—and we looked at every flippin' page—even that had nothin' on it. Hopeful about that I was—phone books often do give you a lead. People will scribble on 'em. But there it is. No one on the other boats in the Basin knew anything about Quayle and this Vickers.

Thought they were just a quiet respectable married couple. Well, I know they weren't *that*. Checked on birth and wedding registrations and Gawd knows what else, and Quayle was married all right—to some woman we can't trace. I feel right up a blind alley, and it's not comfortable.'

The mood of the hospital improved in inverse ratio to Spain's patent discontent. The more sulky he looked because of his inability to get any further with his investigations, the more cheerful everyone else became. Derek Foster looked positively smug because, as he put it, 'I like to see policemen up a gum tree,' and Colin Jackson was much less surly now that the hospital was running along its usual well oiled paths again.

Jeff was still working in the laboratories not because, as he was at some pains to point out to Barney, he had been cleared of any complicity in the blood switching business, but because there was no one else to do his work.

'Pathologists are hard to come by, Barney. Not like anaesthetists. Believe me, if Stroud had someone else to put in my place, he'd suspend me too. I'm really sorry you're lumbered, though.'

'I'll get over it,' Barney had grunted. But it hurt all the same. Work mattered to Barney, mattered a great deal, and enforced idleness didn't suit him in the least.

But he had Lucy, and in that week, their

feeling for each other grew and stretched itself, and developed substance. For Lucy what had started as a simple attraction became, she knew, a life long commitment. Whatever happened, whether she and Barney did decide to spend their lives together (even in her most secret thoughts, she found it difficult to use the word marriage. It seemed like tempting Providence) her own die was cast. No one else would ever mean quite so much to her.

On the last night of her week's sick leave, they had dinner at an hotel that lay long and low beside the river near Maidenhead. They sat under fairy lit trees in a garden at the edge of the water, and ate iced soup and salmon salad and strawberries, and drove back to the hospital in a haze of sheer contentment.

Barney parked the car in the Consultants' car park, not caring at all for protocol, and arm in arm they walked across the courtyard towards the hospital, for Barney had insisted that Lucy should come to the doctors' common room for a goodnight cup of coffee.

'We'll cut through Casualty,' he said, as they made their way across the dark courtyard. 'It'll be quicker—'

He pushed open the rubber edged doors, and stood back to let Lucy through, dropping a kiss on the back of her neck as she passed him.

The waiting room was only partially lit, for it was almost midnight, and no patients were in the department at all. The rows of tubular steel and canvas chairs sat mutely, some with tattered magazines on their seats, and the assorted posters on the walls, appealing for blood donors and Civil Nursing Reserve volunteers and urging mothers to take care of their children's teeth, looked down almost benevolently on them as they walked slowly across the tiled floor.

They had just reached the doors on the far side, the doors that led into the outpatient department and the short cut through to the medical staff quarters, when Lucy heard it, and stopped.

'There's a cat in here, Barney,' she said. 'Listen.'

Barney tilted his head and they stood silent for a moment, and then he laughed.

'You're hearing things—'

'No, I'm not. I distinctly heard a mewing noise—all muffled. It must be old Scatty, from the Pharmacy. The poor old thing's got nowhere to go since the fire. She keeps getting into the oddest places. If she's using one of the trolleys for a bed, Sister Byron'll do her nut. We'd better get the wretched animal out—'

'But—just a minute.' Barney listened again. 'You're right. I heard it too—over by the canteen counter—'

The faint sound had seemed to come from the far corner of the big waiting room, by the little section where the WVS dispensed tea and doorstep sandwiches and chocolate biscuits to

168

waiting patients.

Barney went in front of Lucy, weaving his way through the chairs and peering into the shadows by the stack of extra chairs beside the tea urn.

'Come on, Scatty—come on, you benighted cat. Come out of there. Go and catch mice in the kitchens—' he called softly.

The sound came again, but this time it wasn't a mewing at all.

'Good God,' Barney said, and suddenly crouched down to peer between the back row of the waiting chairs and the counter. 'What the hell—'

Lucy peered over his shoulder, and then pushed quickly past to get closer to the source of the noise.

It was the huddled figure of a woman, and she was lying on the floor, her legs drawn up and her arms clutched round them, her head curving down against her chest. She looked more like a bundle of old clothes than a human being.

Together they lifted her, and made her sit in a chair between them, and she moaned and tried to pull away from them. But Lucy's practised movements made it impossible for her to resist their gentle insistence.

'What's the matter?' Barney asked. 'Are you feeling ill? Tell me what's the matter, and I can help you—I'm a doctor.'

The woman raised her head and looked at

169

him, and then at Lucy, and Lucy drew back, suddenly repelled and shocked.

At first glance, the woman had looked middle aged—about forty or so, but now Lucy could see that she was in fact very young—probably not twenty. But her skin had a greyish colour, and there were red marks on her cheeks, as though she had been scratching at them. Her nose was running slightly, but she didn't seem to notice or care, and her eyes under the wild and unkempt hair stared in an odd fashion. It was a moment or two before Lucy could realise why the eyes looked so strange, but then she recognised the cause. The irises looked huge and very blue in comparison with the tiny black pupil in the centre. It gave her a blank almost blind look.

Suddenly the woman put out a hand and clutched Lucy's. It felt horrid—the skin was wet with perspiration, and the nails were rough and broken, and Lucy had to use a considerable effort of will not to pull her hand away in disgust.

'Doctor?' she said, and the voice was husky, sounding as though it wasn't used very often. 'Doctor? You'll help me, Doctor?'

'I'm a nurse,' Lucy said gently. 'We'll help you, both of us. What's the matter? Won't you explain?'

'I've got to see him, I've got to. It won't take long, but I've got to, you must let me, right now, you—must—'

Suddenly she let go of Lucy's hand, and bent forwards again, clutching at her middle, and again she moaned with the high pitched mewing sound they had heard before. Anxiously Lucy bent over her, and said, 'What is it? Have you a pain? Where?'

The woman nodded, and moaned again, and then straightened up slightly, moving experimentally.

'It hurts,' she whimpered. 'It hurts. I've got to see him. I can't stand this any more—I've got to see him. Let me see him, please. Don't make me go on like this. Let me see him—please—' and again she clutched at Lucy's hand.

'See who?' Barney said, and taking hold of the woman's shoulders gently pulled her round to look at him. 'See who?'

'He's got it, he must have it,' she said, and whimpered again, and again clutched at her middle and cried, and retched.

'Lucy, help me get her on to a trolley. We've got to get her into Cas and take a good look at her—'

They lifted her on to one of the trolleys—and she really was very light and bony under the heavy coat she was wearing—and together pushed her through the waiting room and into the main Casualty room.

Staff Nurse Graham poked her head out of the office door, and stared at them in surprise.

'Hello, Sister! Where did you find a patient?

171

Was she outside? Lord, I'm sorry, but I didn't hear anyone come in—'

'It doesn't matter,' Barney said crisply. 'I want her in a cubicle—right now.'

Nurse Graham scuttled across towards a cubicle and swished open the curtains, and then helped pull the trolley alongside the couch and lift the patient on to it.

With practised hands, she and Lucy began to undress her, and Barney said, 'Put her into a gown, will you? I'll be back in a second—' and went hurrying across to the office.

When he came back, the girl was lying on the couch swathed in a white hospital gown, and rolling her head from side to side on the pillow, whimpering and muttering. 'I've got to see him. Right now—you must let me see him—please—'

'I've sent for Spain,' Barney said, as he pulled off his tweed jacket, and rolled up his sleeves. 'He'll be here in a minute.'

'Why?' Lucy was puzzled. 'What's he wanted for?'

'Because I think this girl might give us the answer to a lot of problems—' He started to examine the girl on the couch, listening to her chest, and then rolling up one sleeve to check her blood pressure. He looked up at Lucy's puzzled face before he put the cuff on the thin arm.

'Come on, love!' he said, and his voice carried a rallying note. 'Surely you've worked

172

it out? Look at this arm—'

It was thin and dirty, and along the inner side of the forearm there were several red and angry looking septic spots—and there were scratches, too. Lucy stared, and then looked quickly at the girl's face, shining in the overhead light because the skin was sweating heavily. She put out her hand, and gently lifted one of the girl's closed eyelids, and looked again at the eye beneath, and took a sharp breath.

'Precisely,' Barney said, and then hooked the stethoscope into his ears again as Nurse Graham swiftly attached the tube on the cuff to the blood pressure gauge on the wall.

After a moment, Barney pulled the stethoscope from his ears so that it dangled round his neck, and grunted as Nurse Graham removed the cuff. Then he leaned over the girl again.

She was still moaning, still rolling her head from side to side, and had her knees drawn up sharply under the red blanket that covered her. But when Barney spoke, very softly, she stopped moaning, and opened her eyes, and turned her head to stare eagerly at him.

'Do you want a fix?'

'What did you say?' she almost whispered it.

'I said, do you want a fix?' Barney repeated.

'Oh, God, yes—*yes*. Please—please, mister, have you got one, please? Now? I got money—I got it tonight—I did, on the docks,

173

please, mister—'

Barney's face hardened as he stared down at her, and then he bit his lip.

'You poor little—I don't want any money. You can have a fix. But I want you to promise two things, first.'

'Yes—yes, yes, yes,' she gabbled. 'Anything at all, only don't make me wait any more, please—please—'

'You've got to tell me who you came here to see, and you've got to promise to come into hospital for treatment. It won't be cold turkey, I promise you, though it won't be nice. But you've got to come all the same—is it a deal?'

'Yes!' she almost shrieked it. 'Yes—now—now, please—'

'Nurse Graham!' Barney said sharply. 'I want an intravenous tray, fast, with fifteen milligrams of heroin.' He turned back to the girl again. 'You're mainlining, aren't you?' and she nodded eagerly.

Nurse Graham brought the tray at the same moment that Spain came pushing through the doors with the faithful Travers close behind.

'What's the flap?' he asked, peering over Barney's shoulder as he swabbed the crook of the girl's elbow, and picked up the prepared syringe. 'Who's this?'

'Hang on,' Barney said, and gently pushed the plunger home. The girl moaned again, and rolled her head, and drew up her knees, but Lucy held her gently and firmly, and the needle

174

didn't move in the vein. When Barney withdrew it and dropped it with a clatter in the dish Nurse Graham held ready for him, they all stood staring down at the girl on the couch.

It seemed to happen so quickly. She began to breathe more deeply, and her whole body seemed to relax, and soften, and somehow look younger again.

Then she turned her head and looked up at Barney a little drowsily, and smiled widely. Her teeth were blackened and ugly, but it was a sweet smile that lifted her face.

'Thanks,' she said huskily.

Barney sat down beside her on the couch, and took one of the thin dirty hands in his own.

'Your turn now, love,' he said gently. 'Come on. Talk. You promised.'

She turned her head away again, but he put out a finger and hooked it under her chin, and made her look at him.

'You promised,' he said, and his tone was crisp and very authoratitive. 'So. Who were you looking for? Your pusher?'

She nodded, a little sulkily.

'Why did you look for him here?'

'Because he told me he was coming here, that's why. Two weeks ago. I got a big supply and he said he'd be back in two weeks but I could get more from the usual place if I needed it. But when I went to the boat tonight there was no one there and—'

'What *is* all this?' Spain said, and for the first

175

time there was real irritation in his voice.

'I'm sorry,' Barney said in a low voice. 'I didn't have time to explain. She's a junkie. A heroin addict. She came here tonight looking for a fix—a dose of heroin—because she was suffering from withdrawal symptoms—and they're damned painful and unpleasant. I made a deal with her—a dose to tide her over in exchange for information. And that's why I wanted you here—to hear it—'

He turned back to the girl. 'Come on, love. Tell me more. *Who* was it? Quayle?'

She whipped her head round and stared at him then. 'If you know, what the bloody hell are you nagging me for? Leave me alone—'

'No, I won't. So, Quayle was your pusher.'

'Yes, he is.' She stopped then, and stared at Barney. 'Did you say *was*?'

Barney nodded, his eyes never leaving her face.

'Quayle's dead,' he said softly. 'He was murdered.'

'Oh, my God,' the girl said, and then started to shake. 'Oh, my God—'

'So, you're in trouble, aren't you? What'll you do now? You'd be much better off to come into hospital for treatment the way you promised you would—'

She laughed suddenly, a shrill laugh. 'Junkie's promises! Who cares for them? I'd say anything to get a fix. Don't you know that?'

'Yes I know. And if you want another when

you come down from this one, you'd better let me have the answers I want. There'll be no help for you otherwise—'

'Barney—' Lucy put her hand out. 'Barney—for pity's sake! You can't treat her this way—giving her more of the drug—'

But he shook his head at her, and returned to the girl, his voice taking on an even harsher note.

'So? What's it to be? Do you tell me?'

There was a short silence, and then she said sulkily, 'Tell you what?'

'What you'll do now your pusher's dead?'

A glint came into her eye, a sly one, and she looked at him under her lashes.

'Get it from the other feller,' she said, and giggled.

'Which other fellow?'

'His supplier. The one here.'

There was a sharp hiss as Spain took a sudden breath, and leaned a little closer.

'Who is he?' he asked in a sharp and rather loud voice. 'Come on—who is he? I'm a policeman, ducky, and if you don't come out with it, I'll take you in—and you know what that means, don't you? So come on. *Who?*'

'I don't bloody well *know!*' the girl shouted back at him. 'But he's here, and I'll find him somehow. Someone'll know, somewhere, one of the crowd. I'll find out—as long as you know where a pusher hangs out, sooner or later you find out who he is. I'll get by. Leave me

177

alone—' and she began to swear with a fluency that overwhelmed even Spain.

'Stop that!' This was Nurse Graham, and she leaned forwards and gave the girl a firm shake of the shoulders. And as suddenly as she had started, the girl stopped, and flopped down again on the couch, and turned her back to them to lie curled up in the babyish position in which Lucy and Barney had first found her.

Spain leaned forwards as though to speak to her again, but Barney shook his head, and pulled him back. Together they came out of the cubicle, with Lucy and the taciturn Sergeant Travers following them, leaving Nurse Graham to look after the girl.

'You won't get any more out of her,' Barney said, and his eyes were very bright as he looked at Spain. 'But I know how we can find out more. And as I see it, find out who was supplying Quayle with his drugs and we've got his murderer.'

'Oh, that's clear enough!' Spain said a little scornfully, and walked across the main Casualty room to Sister's office, the others following him. 'It don't take much to work that out. Quayle was gettin' stuff from one of the staff here, who got fed up and wanted out. And took the best way out he could. I reckon it all happened at once—Quayle gettin' ill enough to come into hospital, and then Bruce findin' out about the thefts. It had to happen sooner or later, o' course. No one gets away with robbery of this sort for very long. So this bloke decides to clean up the mess—and makes a worse one while he was at it.'

'The notebook,' Lucy said suddenly.

'What?' Spain squinted across at her.

'The notebook,' she said again. 'And the brief case. That's what Roberta Vickers was killed for. It must have had something in it about this—supplier, whoever he is. He must have been afraid she'd split on him.'

'Not on your life,' Spain said crisply. 'I daresay you're right enough about the fact the notebook and the brief case held evidence that would point to our man—but the reason that woman was killed is much simpler. I reckon Quayle was a blackmailer—that he had somethin' on this bloke. And got himself paid off in drugs. I mean, if this bloke's a doctor, and I'm sure he is, he's not goin' to risk his career to let someone else make money out of what he steals, is he? O' course not. If he fancies himself in the drug business, he acts as his own pusher. He doesn't split the profits. So, when Quayle got too much for him, he killed him, but didn't reckon to be inherited. But he was, you see. This Roberta Vickers—she must have been up to her eyes in the business. She lived with Quayle, on this boat—the *Bobby Vee*—and you heard that girl just now. She went to the boat for supplies, didn't she? Expectin' to get them from Vickers, that's what. As I see it, when Quayle died Vickers lost no time in tellin'

179

our bloke the situation was just as before, with herself as the recipient, so he killed her too. Makes sense, don't it?'

'It does,' Barney said, and there was an air of suppressed excitement about him. 'And now we've got to find Our Bloke, as you call him. And I know how to do it—'

'Right,' Spain said. 'I'm a reasonable man. Always was. I believe in listenin' to people, if they reckon they know somethin' that might be helpful. Don't promise to do anything about what they say but I'll always listen.' Spain was definitely recovering some of his normal good humour. A small break in the clouds that had overhung his case was quite enough to make him bounce up again.

'We tell the people here about this girl. That we now know there's a drug supplier here, and that she came to see him. We tell people she's in a single room—your side ward perhaps, Lucy—and then sit back and wait.'

Spain frowned. 'A decoy? But why should he bite? She doesn't know who it is.'

'I know she doesn't,' Barney said impatiently. 'But the Bloke must be led to think she does. Look, if I go to breakfast tomorrow, when everyone is there, and tell this story, dropping in, ever so casually, that the patient said she knew who it was, but then passed out, and we're just waiting for her to come round so that you can talk to her and close the case, what'll happen?'

180

'He'll panic,' Spain said slowly.

'Of course he will. He'll try to get at her, and kill her. I mean, he's demolished three people. What's one more to someone like that?'

'And we'll be waiting for him.'

'But of course!' Barney said.' Isn't it always done in the best of police circles? The setting of traps? The using of decoys? I thought that was all policewomen were ever used for.'

'Hmmph,' Spain said. 'You're gettin' cheeky. But if we do it, one thing's sure. We'll have to use a policewoman in the room. You can't use the real junkie, can you?'

'I wouldn't dream of it!' Barney said. 'She's a sick girl and needs treatment. No, we'll get her admitted to the psychiatric unit tomorrow, down in Surrey. The policewoman idea's fine. Are we on?'

There was a silence. They stood there, Lucy close beside Barney, staring up at him, Travers leaning against the wall and staring fixedly but woodenly at his chief, and Spain sitting perched on Sister's desk, turning a paper knife in his heavy hands, his chin sunk into his neck.

Lucy could hear the hiss and splutter of the steam sterilisers outside in the main room, and the distant roar of traffic from the road far beyond, and the faint clutter of sterilising drums as far down the corridors a porter made his last round of the wards. And then Spain broke the spell, lifting his head and looking at Barney with his eyes very sharp and bright, filled almost with pleasure.

'Yes. We're on. We should be able to make an arrest by this time tomorrow. We'll get it up right now.'

CHAPTER TWELVE

She could see the ward quite clearly from her office. The glass partition sparkled a little in the light from her desk lamp, throwing back the reflection of her own figure at the desk. She could see quite clearly the pin on the breast of her apron, the frills on her cap, the very white line of her starched collar against her suntanned throat. It made her feel a little unreal, sitting there staring at her own reflection etched against the rows of beds in the ward itself, marching into the night-time shadows, with the clock face at the far end of the ward gleaming through the darkness above her head. Three a.m. it read. The shank of the night, but Lucy was too keyed up to be sleepy.

Somewhere near the far end, a patient called hoarsely, and Lucy saw the night nurse rise swiftly from her chair under the shaded light in the centre of the ward and go hurrying silentfootedly away. Then there was a swathe of light across the polished floor and a faint clatter. The patient wanted a bedpan, Lucy thought automatically, and then turned her head to look through her office door to the side-ward door beyond.

It was as blank and still as it had been the last time she had looked at it, a few moments ago. Behind it lay the little blonde policewoman, lying in the bed with a mock up of an intravenous drip attached to her arm, and her head turned into the shadows of the pillow. A brave woman, thought Lucy, and shivered. Not that there was anything to be scared of. Was there?

She pulled her cape closer round her shoulders and tried to reassure herself. Spain had assured her all would be well, when the whole thing had been planned.

'I'm not askin' no permission for this, Sister, except from you. It's your ward, and you can give it, I know that. But if I go to Stroud, or the Matron or someone, and say I want to plant a decoy in one of the wards, and surround it with a lot of coppers, there'll be all hell let loose. And what's more, it'll be all over the hospital in no time at all, and everyone'll know there's a trap laid up on Female Medical—includin' our bloke. So let's keep quiet about it, eh? It's really the best way.'

And, worriedly, she had agreed, since Barney too had done his best to persuade her. It went against all her nursing instincts to allow her ward to be used as a trap, her ward full of patients.

But Barney had said, 'It means a lot to me,

183

Lucy. Until this is cleared up, I'm a suspended character, with the suspicion of murder or negligence or whatever hanging over me. And there's no danger, you know. That's a policewoman in there—not a real patient. She won't come to harm—she's trained to look after herself. I've set it all up now, sweetheart. You must let us do it—'

Barney had done a very good job that morning, by all accounts. He had gone into breakfast deliberately late, when everyone was there, and before any of them had had a chance to go. He had told, with much graphic detail, the story of the arrival of the drug addict in Casualty the night before, and told them that she had said she knew the name of the person who had been getting drugs from the Pharmacy.

'She's in the side-ward on Female Medical,' he'd gone on with a nicely graduated performance of casualness as he helped himself to scrambled eggs and kippers.

'Once she's a bit less dehydrated and we can get some sense out of her, we're home and dry—or so Spain says. He's confident he can make an arrest some time soon.'

There had been a sharp silence, and then Jackson had said sourly, 'And about time too. The time that man has wasted here—sooner it's cleared up the better.'

'Absolutely,' Harry Caspar had murmured, staring at Barney.

184

Hickson had said nothing, just listening with his usual hangdog expression on his face, but when Barney caught his eyes, and became aware of the glint in their depths, he wondered. Could Hickson be quite as much of a fool as he seemed?

And as for the others—Derek Foster had laughed and said, 'Good oh—I'm getting tired of falling over coppers wherever I go. It's cramping my love life.'

Jeff had grunted in his usual fashion, but then grinned at Barney and said, 'It'll be good to get back to work, eh, Barney?' and Barney had warmed to him. Jeff operated on much the same level as he did himself when it came to work. It mattered deeply to Jeff, just as it did to Barney, and of all of them, perhaps only Jeff really knew how he had felt these past miserable workless days.

'Though I know you understand too, Lucy,' Barney had finished, when he explained all this to her. 'But—well, it's different, *your* understanding. All mixed up with other things.' And then he'd kissed her and said wheedlingly, 'You will co-operate, Lucy?' So what could she do?

There was a faint draught suddenly, whispering round the corner of the door, and nervously, Lucy pulled the desk phone a little nearer. Her job was a very simple one. She was to sit here, and if she saw anything at all odd, no matter how small, she was to lift the

185

receiver. That was all—just lift it and put it on the desk. The policeman who was planted on the switchboard in place of the usual man would then raise the alarm and send half the local constabulary streaming out of their assorted hiding places in the vicinity of Female Medical to her side-ward. It was all so simple— and so safe, she reminded herself, but without any real conviction.

I wonder how she is in there? she thought, as the draught came whispering again. Such a nice girl, pert and cheeky, almost a feminine version of Spain, with her sharp tongue and friendly eyes. Was she scared? Or was she so used to such assignments that she'd dropped off to sleep? And why not? Spain had sworn his men would get any intruder long before he could reach the bedside—

And then she knew. Knew that the draughts she had felt hadn't been merely accidental. Someone had opened the big outer doors, had stood there silently listening, and then just as softly closed them again—with himself on the inside. She could feel the presence of this alien somebody, almost hear his soft breathing, feel the warmth of his body.

Stiffly she turned her head, to look up the ward, suddenly wanting to see the comforting figure of the night nurse. But she was still occupied with the patient in the far corner. Only sleeping patients lay between her and the stranger within her doors. Only Lucy herself and the stranger were awake.

And then she remembered the policemen hiding around, the one in the linen cupboard, crouching absurdly among the blankets and the piles of sheets and pillow slips, the one behind the kitchen door, the other one in the main store cupboard, and breathed again. And there was Barney, too, inside that room with Spain and two other policemen as well as Travers, all silent behind the screens in the corner, waiting to get their man before he could do any harm to the cheeky blonde in the bed.

It was as though she were psychic. She couldn't hear him, couldn't see him, but she knew he was moving nearer, along the short corridor between the main double doors and the ward doors, could feel his presence getting bigger and more ominous. Slowly she stretched out her hands to the phone, let it rest on the handpiece, and strained her eyes towards the blank polished panels of the side-ward door.

She saw his shadow first, incredibly elongated in the dim light of the corridor, touching the door, climbing up and across it, distorted and ugly. And she sat there, frozen, unable to move a muscle, so sick was she with fear, so paralysed with terror.

And then she saw him. A square shape, absurdly square and solid, human and yet somehow not, with a blank face and a perfectly smooth round head and smooth very dark brown hands. A monstrous creature.

And then she heard an hysterical giggle deep inside her as she saw why the figure looked so strange. Theatre rig. He was wearing theatre clothes, a dark green gown over heavy but silent-treading white rubber boots, smooth dark brown rubber gloves giving his hands the exaggerated elegance of a shop window dummy, a tight dark green cap, and a broad white mask that covered his face from lower lashes to neck.

She couldn't see his eyes properly, for his face was turned towards the door, and one hand was slowly, so slowly, turning the handle.

But still she sat, unable to move, and the door opened wider and wider and then he was gone, slipping inside like a wraith in the half light of the corridor—

At the far end of the ward water flushed suddenly as a tap was turned on, and it broke the spell. Convulsively she grabbed the phone and let the handpiece clatter to the desk, and then she was on her feet, hurling herself at the door. They had told her to stay in her office, no matter what happened, but she couldn't do that, not now that she had let them down so badly. The alarm should have been called as soon as that shadow had appeared, and she had wasted valuable seconds because she had been too frightened to move.

It all seemed to happen at once. As she reached the side-ward door, there was a sudden furious clatter, and her mind said with precise and nurselike tones, 'They've knocked over the screens—'

And then the door burst open, and the green gowned figure shot out, with four others behind him, but the figure saw her, standing right across his way, and seized her in an incredibly hard grip and whirled her round, and held her against him as he looked over her shoulder at the four men.

She saw Barney's face whiten, saw him drop back, saw the others look sick and frightened, and dropped her own eyes to look in terror at the hand that was clamping her so firmly to the hard chest behind her.

It glittered, almost prettily, with a light of its own. A bone scalpel, wickedly long and sharp, with an edge that would split a hair, and it was pressed against her own chest, pressed so firmly that she could see a deep slit in the starched front of her apron.

In the brief moment, when the four men stood staring in the same sort of paralysed stupefaction she had felt herself, the green gowned figure moved, and moved her with him as though she were no more than a doll.

He moved, in fact, backwards, without any fear, obviously knowing where he was going. She felt him fumble behind himself, felt the sharp cold air as the door swung wide. The balcony, she thought, the balcony and the fire escape.

And then they were out there, out on the cracked tiles of the old balcony, leaning against the rusty iron rails by the fire escape.

He pulled on her, pulled hard, forcing her to cling to the railings, and then, swinging behind her, put his own feet on the first of the narrow fire escape stairs, and pulled her with him.

She looked up, as she felt the inexorable tug of one gloved hand on her waist, and saw Barney's face peering down at her from the balcony now receding further and further above her, for she was obediently climbing downwards, letting the anonymous figure in the gown guide her. She had no choice, for when she hesitated, even for a second, she felt the edge of the knife against her forearm, the one she was using to try to fend off the gloved hand. And he meant his silent gestures with that knife, she discovered, for when she hesitated momentarily, the knife rested against her skin and she felt a sudden cold-hot pain, and a warm trickle of blood drifted down towards her fingers.

It became nightmarish. She could hear shouts, and there were lights swooping and dancing, always somehow missing the man who held her in his nutcracker grip. They began to climb again and then went scuttling across some wide open space, and then slithered down a rough incline, and she could smell soot and smoke in the cold early morning air.

And the man who pushed and tugged her along, holding his scalpel constantly against her, filling her with fear of its icy edge, made no sound, spoke not one syllable, not even a grunt.

But she knew he was feeling the strain, could tell by his harsher breathing, and the now and then clumsy movement that betrayed fatigue. She tried to turn her head once, tried to look in his face, but he pushed her head back with such roughness that it made her neck snap, made her feel a sudden sick surge of pain. She didn't try again.

And then he stopped, and let go of her, and she fell to her knees, to half kneel, half lie, on the rough surface of wherever it was, as she gulped for breath, her terror and the sheer physical effort she had been forced to make robbing her of any feeling but the desperate need to rest.

But after a moment or two she raised her head, and looked up. The gowned figure was bending over a parapet, peering downwards, and she raised herself slowly and awkwardly till she was standing on her feet.

She could see them, quite clearly. Seven storeys below, the courtyard was alive with lights, dancing and sweeping across and upwards, but the overhang of the children's ward balcony just below cut off the beams that were directed upwards, so they were hidden from the glare.

She turned her head and could see, on the far side of their rooftop—for they were out on the flat leads in the lee of one of the tall ventilation shaft housings that starred the main block of the hospital—the lights of the docks and the faint oily gleam of the river, and the soaring lovely iron lace of dockside cranes.

She had her bearings now. He had managed to pull her from the second floor balcony sideways, across to the transport office roof, up across the engineers' department, to this vantage point on the roof of the main building. Obviously the searchers hadn't realised, hadn't dreamed, that their quarry would go upwards again, after dropping down the fire escape as he had. She was up here, alone on a roof seven storeys above the ground, with a murderer. And no one knew where she was, or was within shouting reach.

He straightened up then, and turned, and she shrank back against the ventilator housing, fear rising high in her throat. She saw the glint of his eyes above the faint white glimmer of the mask, and something about them made her think, wildly, 'But I know you—it's—' and then he moved and the moment of recognition went, melting into her fear, and she didn't know who it was who had covered his escape to this far roof by dragging her with him, found nothing familiar in the body that bulked under the green gown, the shape of the head under the tight fitting cap.

192

'Please—' she didn't realise for a moment that it was her own voice, hardly realised she had anything to say. 'Please let me go—'

The figure turned and stood very still for a second and then shook its head, and moved towards her again, and she pulled away, scuttled round the side of the ventilator shaft housing in the sort of terror that makes an animal run even when it knows there is no escape.

'No—no, please, whoever you are—please, no—'

The figure stopped then, suddenly, and again she caught the faint glitter in the eyes, as they looked at her. And almost instinctively she knew what to say, what the brain behind the mask and cap was weighing up.

'I don't know who you are,' she said breathlessly, and her words were snatched from her mouth by a gust of wind and tossed back like an echo. 'I don't know—no one knows—not the addict, no one. Let me go, please—let me go—'

The conviction in her voice was intense. She knew that, listening to herself in a queerly objective fashion, feeling her own hands as they clung to the wood of her perch, feeling the ache in her arm where she had been cut.

And it did convince him, for he turned then, and moved away from her, back towards the coping at the edge of the roof.

She watched him almost in a dream, saw him

leaning over the coping, looking downwards, was aware of the careful consideration he was giving to the situation. And as she leaned, spent and sick, against the frail wooden planks she became aware of something else, and watched almost casually, almost as though it didn't concern her.

She saw first one head appear, and then another, over the edge of the roof on the far side, the engineers' department side, the way she and her captor had come themselves. She saw them move, become part of total figures, saw them come closer to the figure that leaned so thoughtfully over the edge of the parapet. She saw that one of the silent stalking figures was Barney and wanted to call his name, to show herself at him, but again she couldn't move. She just stood there breathing painfully and deeply and watching in a state of remoteness.

It happened with the inevitability of an organised beautifully choreographed ballet. As the leader of the two figures—Spain? yes, Spain—hurled itself forwards, towards the rubber booted legs of the figure by the coping, the figure turned, and saw, and moved sideways sharply, swinging out with one leg at the head of his nearest assailant. But he missed, and swung there wildly on one leg for a moment, silhouetted in mad pattern against the sky, and then he fell. And there was a thick cracking sound as he hit something.

Lucy thought he had gone over the edge, so sharply did the silhouette disappear, and the shock of the idea brought movement back to her. She flung herself forwards, and shrieked, 'Barney!' and he was there and caught her, and held her very close and tight and she put her face against his chest and went on saying, 'Barney—', but more softly, with a sense of safety and peace that she had forgotten could exist.

But Barney moved after a few moments, and with one arm held protectively round her moved over towards the huddle of figures by the coping, for more men had arrived, more black shadows bulking against the lesser blackness that was the sky.

A light danced, and Lucy saw Spain's capable square fingered hands move forwards, saw the huddled figure of the gowned man against the coping, saw the light shift, and fix itself on the face.

Spain put his hand out further, and hooked one finger over the top of the mask, and pulled it downwards, over the nose, so that it hooked under the chin like some incongruous ruff.

The eyes were half open, and staring bleakly upwards, and the face was quite blank. It was odd to see him lying there like that, so blank and silent, Lucy thought vaguely, letting all these people hang over him, staring at him like this, pulling him about. Not like Jeff Heath at all.

195

CHAPTER THIRTEEN

She had been crying, but now she felt better, though her eyes were hot and swollen, and her throat hurt because of the way she had held it constricted trying to keep the stupid tears back. But now she felt better, and warmer too, for she had been so cold.

It was daylight now, broad daylight, and the hospital was bustling and moving around her. She could hear the distant clatter of bowls and basins as the night nurses did the morning's rounds of washings and dressings, could smell the distant fragrance of bacon and toast as the kitchens got into gear for breakfasts which would have to be served in half an hour. It was six-thirty, and the day's work was well under way.

The door swung open, and the night nurse came in, and smiled at her.

'I brought you some breakfast, Sister. Nothing much—just a boiled egg and some toast and tea but you need it—'

'I couldn't—' Lucy said a little fretfully, but the girl took no notice.

'You could have it in the office if you'd rather. It's a bit lonely in the side-ward here—'

'Oh—well, thanks, I'll stay here, I think. I must look an incredible mess, and I'd hate the patients to see me like this.'

'You don't look your normal self, I must say,' the night nurse said cheerfully. 'So have it here. Now, Sister, if you want any more, just give me a ring, will you? I'm just doing breakfasts in the kitchen, so I won't be far away—'

'Thanks awfully,' Lucy said and smiled gratefully at her. 'You're very good—all I want now is Bar—Dr Elliot and some *news*. Will you watch out for him and send him straight in here?'

And the night nurse nodded and went away, leaving Lucy to her breakfast and her shakiness, for she still felt decidedly unlike her usual self.

It had all been such a hubbub. Spain and his men had started to pick up Jeff, to get him down from the roof, but he had come round from the blow on his head, and started to fight back with a sort of despairing violence that distressed Lucy more than she would have thought possible. But they had controlled him—of course they had. There had been a good half dozen men against him. What hope had he had?

And then Barney had led her away, carefully guiding her feet down the long swaying fire escape to the courtyard far below, and she had clung to him, and wept, and she didn't know whether it was because it was all over, or because she had been so frightened before, or because it had been Jeff, for Jeff had been a sort of friend, and she had liked him—

They had cleaned her arm and dressed it in Casualty, after putting several stitches in the gaping wound, and she had watched Colin Jackson's flat careful fingers putting them in and told herself over and over again, '—Jeff did this. He would have killed me, if he'd felt he had to, just as he killed those other people. Three people he killed, and would have killed again. *Jeff* did this—' But she couldn't really believe it.

Colin Jackson had insisted she go and rest, and when she had flatly refused to go to the Staff sick bay had grudgingly agreed she could go to her own side-ward, for the policewoman had left it now and she could rest there for a few hours.

Barney had promised to come to her, as soon as he could.

'But I've got to find out what's what, Lucy,' he had said sombrely. 'Jeff is—was, I suppose, now—my friend. I've got to go and find out. I'll be back, Lucy—'

And she had wept, and then dozed fitfully and then woken and wept again, and now she felt a little better. And the toast smelled good and the satiny brown shell of the egg on the prettily laid tray did look inviting—

She ate everything, all the toast, and the last scrapings of marmalade and butter and emptied the teapot completely. And as she poured the last cupful and liberally sugared it,

198

the door opened and Barney came in.

She looked up at his white face with the heavy violet shadows under the grey eyes, and mutely held out the cup and saucer to him. He sketched a smile at her, and took it, and drank greedily, saying nothing.

The little night nurse put her head round the door, and nodded approvingly and went away to come back with another egg and more toast and marmalade, and another pot of tea and he in his turn demolished a big breakfast, as they sat in companionable silence.

Watching him, his squared shoulders hunched a little over the tray he held on his lap as he sat there in the big armchair opposite her own, she felt warm and safe again. The fear of the night, the misery of the morning caused by the knowledge that Jeff, their friend Jeff, had been the man Spain had jocularly called 'our Bloke' and caught like a rat in a trap, all evaporated. While Barney was there, all was very right in Lucy's world.

He looked up then, and caught her eye, and smiled at her, and she saw a smudge of yellow egg yolk on his chin, and she felt tears of sheer happiness boil up in her throat.

'Oh, Barney!' she said, and the tears spilled over and smudged her dirty cheeks. 'Oh, Barney, I do love you so much.'

He put the tray down on the floor, and lifted his weary body from the chair, and came over to her, and she stood up, and put her arms

199

round his neck, and kissed his tired eyes and big eggy chin and stubbled cheeks and then his warm mouth, and wept again, and laughed too. And Barney laughed too, a soft excited sort of laugh and held her very close and kissed her till she was breathless.

Then he sat down again, and pulled her down to sit curled on his lap, her head fitting comfortably into the curve where his neck met his shoulder. They sat in silence for a long time, and then Lucy said, almost dreamily, 'What happened? What did you find out?'

He moved then, uncomfortably, and she put out a hand and stroked the arm that was resting around her, and he relaxed again. But when he spoke his voice was sombre.

'He talked a lot, down there in Cas. I've never heard him talk so much. Just went on and on, and that bloody Spain just stood there and stared at him as though—as though he were a specimen on a slab. It was funny. It was just the sort of look I've seen on Jeff's face when he was doing a post mortem. Remote, you know? Academically interested, but not thinking about the—the body he was working on as though it had once been a person. I wonder. Maybe it was because of being a pathologist that he could do it?'

'What?' Lucy was bewildered.

'I'm sorry—I went off at a tangent. I mean, I wonder if it was because Jeff was a pathologist that he could be a murderer? Path people—

they spend so much time dealing with specimens and bodies—maybe they lose their feeling for people as people—I don't know—'

'He did do it all then,' Lucy said flatly. 'I've been sort of hoping that—'

'That it wasn't him, even though he sprang the trap. I know. I felt the same. But it was him. It's—sickening isn't it? A friend—'

He seemed to brood for a moment and then said with a defensive sort of note in his voice, 'Not that he could help it, really. Oh, hell—that's stupid. Of course he could help it. What I mean is, he had tremendous provocation.'

'Can you tell me about it? Or don't you want to talk about it anymore?' It was odd how attuned she felt to Barney's feelings. She felt a reluctance in him to talk about it but at the same time a sort of need to get the information out, into the air.

'Of course I'll tell you about it,' Barney said after a moment. 'Though it's hard to know where to start.' He sat very still for a long pause, thinking, then he said, 'It goes back a long way, really. Jeff's not a natural born doctor type—I mean, there was no family tradition of academic success, or work that involved helping people. No family at all, to speak of. His parents were divorced just before his birth apparently, and there was never much effort made to hide from him the fact that he was unwanted—had never been wanted. His father never saw him, and his mother had done

201

her damnedest to get rid of him, both before he was born and afterwards. Can you imagine what sort of a mother would actually tell her child a thing like that? Anyway, she did—frequently. He had a lousy time as a child.

'But he was bright—well, we all knew that—and worked like a crazy thing at school, and scraped and saved and got himself to University and then medical school, working as a waiter and a navvy and Lord knows what else. It was extraordinary, Lucy. I've known him all this time and I never knew a thing *about* him. He was just taciturn old Jeff who never said much to anyone—and this morning, down there in Cas., he talked and talked as though he couldn't stop. It all came pouring out—

'Anyway, he was doing his first houseman job—and that was in Pathology, because he said he never really liked people all that much. He always preferred the—the separateness of the laboratory—that was how he put it, the separateness—well, he was working there, and one of the secretaries in the department got pregnant. Spain asked Jeff if it was his doing—' Barney's face darkened. 'Of course, only Spain would ask a question like that.'

'Be fair Barney. He has to do his job,' Lucy said a little weakly, but Barney ignored that.

'Anyway, she asked Jeff to abort her. He didn't want to—not because he had specially strong opposition views on abortion, but because he just didn't want to get involved. But she went on and on at him, and said what sort of life would the baby have anyway, illegitimate and completely unwanted—and apparently it was that that sparked a response in him. The woman had hit on the one thing that could make Jeff do as she wanted.

'Well, he agreed. He agreed to go to her flat one evening and aborted her—or attempted to. The thing was, she wasn't pregnant—'

'What?'

'That's right. She wasn't pregnant. Poor Jeff—you have to pity him. The poor devil had taken the woman at her word, and believed her. Anyway, he was furious when he discovered it—as much with himself for not taking steps to be sure she was pregnant before he agreed to meddle with her—and then she told him why. She'd provided a witness—had him hiding in the room, and he'd seen the whole thing—and had a tape recording. It was a frame-up—isn't that the term? A frame-up.'

'But *why*?'

'Drugs,' Barney said succinctly. 'The witness was Quayle—and the woman who wanted aborting though she wasn't pregnant was Roberta Vickers.'

'Oh my God,' Lucy said, and felt a sudden twist of pity for Jeff that made her want to cry again.

'He had a thriving drug-pushing set up already,' Barney said bitterly. 'But something had broken his supply line. And his girl friend was working in a hospital, so between them they cooked up this scheme. This all started five or six years ago—'

'Has—had Jeff been involved with them all this time?'

'Oh, yes. It wasn't money they wanted for their blackmail. Nothing so simple—they knew that wouldn't do them any good because Jeff hadn't got any. A resident's pay doesn't go far.

'Anyway, he paid up what they did want. He systematically stole drugs for them, heroin, cocaine, some morphia and a lot of amphetamine. And they got richer and richer and he got more and more desperate. Of course he's been lucky to get away with it all this time, but he's had four resident posts in the time, and he got out of each hospital long before anyone spotted what was going on—but here it was different. He stayed here longer than he'd ever been anywhere else because the Royal was his own medical school—and he had a chance of a better job. Old Simon Towers—the senior consultant pathologist—he retires next year. There was every likelihood of Jeff getting the post. Well, we all *knew* he would. He's a bloody marvellous pathologist and it was a foregone conclusion he'd get the job.'

'And that meant he had to stop his drug stealing—' Lucy said.

'Of course. He's no fool—he knew someone'd spot it sooner or later. And when

204

Quayle developed an ulcer, he had his chance. He told Quayle to come and see Sir James, made sure he'd be admitted here, and worked out how to get rid of him. Only it all went wrong.'

'You'd think Quayle would have more sense than to come so near someone so—someone who hated him so much. He put himself in a very vulnerable position, didn't he?'

'I thought that too—and I said so to Jeff this morning. He's an extraordinarily clear-eyed bloke in some ways, you know. He said Quayle saw him as two people—the drug thief he employed was one of them, and as such to be—well, manipulated, despised, used as Quayle saw fit. But Jeff was still a *doctor*—and Quayle had that rather naïve attitude to doctors so many lay people have. That doctors aren't like ordinary people when they're doing their doctoring. Am I explaining this properly? I hope I am—but it just never occurred to Quayle that Jeff, in his doctor's hat, could bring himself to harm a patient—even if that patient were blackmailing him. And there was another thing, Jeff said. Quayle saw nothing intrinsically *wrong* in what he did, or what he made other people do in order to satisfy his needs. From his point of view, the blackmailing of Jeff was a straight business deal and just didn't affect Jeff as a doctor.' Barney shivered slightly. 'Quayle really was a revolting man. He deserved what happened to him—'

'You can't say that, Barney. However awful someone is, they—well, they have their reasons. People who didn't know would say Jeff was a terrible person for doing what he did. But he had his reasons.'

'I suppose so. Anyway, there it is. It was Jeff who filled an ampoule with insulin and planted it in theatre. Jeff who changed the blood—and who else could it have been? If we'd thought about it logically we'd have known. Who else understood the lab and the transfusion system and the crossmatching set-up as well as Jeff did? No one!'

'It was all him—the fire in the Pharmacy, and Roberta Vickers—all of it?' Lucy asked.

'Of course it was. He was the only person who had any reason to do those things. As soon as he heard that Bruce wanted to see Stroud, he knew why. He told Spain that he decided right then what to do. And he cleared the drugs from the safe, set fire to the place, and then came over to the "Ship in Bottle" looking for an alibi. And found us.'

'But he couldn't know we'd be there—'

'He knew *someone* would. Is there ever a time when there isn't someone from the hospital in the saloon bar? He just had to talk to anyone who knew him, and be there when the alarm went up. It never occurred to us that he started the fire, did it? Because he was with us! The point is, it takes some time for a fire to get established. He had plenty of time to get over to the "Ship in Bottle"'.

Lucy was thinking. 'But, Barney—about the Vickers woman. If she was part of the drug business from the start, surely he knew she'd take over from Quayle. What was the point of killing Quayle when she'd just carry on where he left off?'

Barney grimaced slightly. 'Jeff—he was quite calm and explicit about that. Spain asked him the same question. He'd intended to kill her too, from the start. He hadn't given much thought to how or when. He just intended to grab whatever chance came along. He'd waited so many years—another few days made no odds. And then he said, "who'd connect me with the death of a woman like that, any more than they'd connect me with the death of Quayle? I was never seen with either of them, after that first start, years ago. I'd probably have gone to the boat, to get rid of her, when it suited me. But she made it easy for me."'

'What did he mean by that?'

'Quayle carried all his most valuable possessions with him—and one of the most valuable was the tape recording that kept Jeff working for him, and the lists of people who worked as intermediate pushers for him, and the names of those he supplied—addicts. He took those into hospital with him, in the brief case.'

'But *why*?' Lucy said quickly. 'Why on earth
207

bring things that were as valuable as that into hospital? Wouldn't it have been safer to have left them locked up at home—on his houseboat? It seems such a stupid thing to have done.'

'On the face of it, maybe—especially when you remember that for part of his time in hospital he'd be out cold, under an anaesthetic. Spain thought of that too, but there *was* a reason for it—a damned good one from Quayle's point of view,' Barney said. 'It was the Vickers woman, you see. They lived together—had done for years, according to Jeff—but as a relationship it was more of an armed neutrality than a real partnership. Quayle was always very careful not to let Vickers get her hands on anything really important, even though he used her as a lieutenant when he needed to. And he just couldn't trust her not to walk off with the whole bit while he was in hospital—drug sources, pushers, addicts, the lot. So, he kept those valuables with him. Apparently he consigned the brief case to Sister Palmer's care while he was in theatre, and demanded it back as soon as he came round from his anaesthetic. Not that he had it for long after that, of course, because he died—'

Barney stopped and took a deep breath, and then he went on.

'Anyway, what happened was this. After Quayle's death, Jeff contacted the Vickers woman and told her he had a fresh supply of stuff for her. Remember—he'd taken a huge load from the safe before starting the fire. He arranged to meet her in the hospital garden to hand the stuff over. She told him she was going to collect the brief case—knowing damned well that only she could be given it, since Quayle had had to designate her as his next of kin—and told Jeff that she strongly suspected he'd had something to do with Quayle's death. However, she didn't care about that except that it made her stronger—better able to blackmail Jeff, and she wanted Jeff to know she now owned the evidence that could get him struck off—the abortion tape recording—and he was no better off.

'He talked about her so oddly. Almost as though he admired her, I think. Maybe it was because she was a chilly woman—didn't care about Quayle's death, though she'd lived with him for so many years. I think he approved of that.

'Anyway, he came over to the "Ship in Bottle", again to establish an alibi, just in case he needed it, and found us again. I imagine he got a bit of a shock when he heard we were going over to talk to Roberta Vickers, but he didn't show it. Anyway, he had nothing to lose. He told me that. He knew perfectly well Vickers wouldn't tell us anything. Why should she? She'd inherited a rich business and she'd do nothing to jeopardise that.

'Jeff left the "Ship in Bottle" just after us to wait for Vickers by the burnt-out Pharmacy—that was the arrangement.' Barney swallowed hard.

'He killed her with one of the big scalpels from the lab—but before he could get away with the brief case we turned up, and he just crouched there behind the roses—and got away with it. He said he felt around in the brief case while we were there—he had incredibly calm nerves, hadn't he?—and realised the notebook, the one that listed all suppliers and addicts, was missing.

'And then he saw it—by Roberta Vickers' bag. She must have taken it from the brief case to put it in her bag. And he had to have it, because his name was in it, and details of every drug he'd ever supplied. It was all part of Quayle's hold on him. When you put out the lighter, he grabbed. It was just bad luck you spotted him, because he didn't want to hurt you, he said. If you hadn't rushed at him there in the bushes, he'd never have hit you. He—he asked me to tell you he was sorry.'

There was a pause, and then Lucy said, 'I believe he was. He—he could have killed me, you know, up there on the roof this morning. He just had to throw me over the edge of the parapet. But he didn't.'

'I ought to hate him I suppose. He hurt you, he killed people—but I can't. I always thought of him as a friend of mine, and you can't stop

210

feeling that way, just like that. I liked him. I think I always shall,' and Barney finished on a defiant note.

'I shall too,' Lucy said, and lifted her head to kiss him back to a happier frame of mind.

The door clattered and swung open, and they both jumped guiltily, Lucy awkwardly, for her whole body was aching from the night's exploits.

'Oh, don't mind me, you two! I jus' came to collect a few bits of gear I left here,' Spain said, and picked up a small brief case from the corner where the screen had stood. 'Feelin' more the thing now, Sister?'

'Yes, thank you,' Lucy said stiffly.

'Good—Delighted to hear it. I must say, I never knew you hospital people had such a high old time of it!' He stood beside the door, grinning at them, with his hat tipped to the back of his head, the brief case under one arm, and his hands in his trousers pockets. He looked as fresh as though he had had a good night's sleep, apart from the shadowy growth of hair on his cheeks, and his eyes glinted a little wickedly as he looked at them.

'There's you two, staring at each other with your eyes full of romantic longings at every turn, and this feller Hickson skulkin' round the Nurses' Home and makin' a right charlie of himself over some staff nurse—I wish I could join in the fun.'

'Really?' Barney said, his voice a little chilly.

'Well, it would be nice for me, wouldn't it? Never mind, though. I'll just have to battle on with Sergeant Travers to hold *my* hand.' He grimaced slightly. 'Still, it hasn't been all headaches this job, though there were enough. But I'm happy with the outcome—very happy. Got a drug ring nicely tidied up, we have. I'm very popular with our narcotics people this morning, I can tell you—when I phoned in a report, well, you'd have thought I'd copped the last of the Train Robbers, they're so pleased with me—nice finish, isn't it?'

'Is it?' Barney said harshly. 'Nice for you, maybe. But the man you've arrested happens to be a friend of ours. Forgive us if we don't share your elation—'

Spain looked at him for a long time, and then sighed suddenly, a little gusty sigh.

'You're still very young, aren't you, Dr Elliot? Yes. Well, one day you'll find out. It doesn't do, gettin' too involved with individuals. You've got to look beyond 'em, to the other people behind. An awful lot of helpless devils have had their lives ruined by your friend Dr Heath. I know he was blackmailed, I know he was framed—I know all that. But he's been stealin' drugs that have a terrible effect on people. That's why I'm glad I got him—not because of the murders he did. They were bad enough, I grant you, but people who get murdered usually ask for it—Quayle and that Vickers woman, they were ideal

212

murderees if ever I saw 'em. The sailor—that was damned rotten luck. But just remember, Dr Elliot, next time you feel inclined to pity your Dr Jeffrey Heath, and hate me for coppin' him, just you remember that he was part of a drug ring, and that he would have let you carry the can back for him if you'd been arrested for that sailor's death. Just you remember that poor little bitch who came into Casualty the night before last, and the state she was in because of the drugs your precious friend got for her, and think again—'

There was a silence and then Barney nodded briefly.

'I'm sorry,' he said, and Spain smiled again, and held out his hand.

'Goodbye, Dr Elliot. It's been good knowin' you, believe me. And your charming girl.' Spain turned to Lucy, and shook hands with her too. 'You're a right little cracker, aren't you? Cuddly. Yes. Just my type.' He sounded a little regretful. 'Never mind. Be sure an' ask me to your weddin'!'

And then he was gone, and without speaking they went to the window and stood there in silence, watching the courtyard below. It was five minutes before he appeared, a little foreshortened by the angle at which they were looking at him, and he went across the courtyard with his characteristic marching swagger, and climbed into the official looking black car parked by the outpatient block.

213

He looked up just before sitting down, and waved up at them, and then the car door slammed, and the engine started and the car curved and swept away through the Casualty entrance.

The courtyard bustled, as it always did at this time of the morning with day staff coming on duty, and early arrivals for the outpatient department, and surgeons with early lists coming to park their expensive vehicles in their own special corner.

Barney and Lucy stood at the side-ward window, staring down at the activity, hand in hand, and already the memories of the night that had just passed, and the days that had led up to it, began to dwindle and lose importance.

They saw Colin Jackson emerge from the Casualty entrance and bustle across to the transport office, a wad of papers in his hand, and even from this distance they were aware of the tension in him, the urgent need to have everything exactly organised and running with perfect smoothness—his idea of perfect smoothness. Lucy smiled briefly as she saw him, and Barney grinned back at her.

'He's right, you know,' he said softly. 'He really is absolutely right.'

'Spain? About Jeff, you mean? I suppose he is.'

'About that—yes, I think he probably is too. No, what I meant was what he said about you. You *are* a right little cracker—and *very* cuddly.

214

Have I told you I love you?'

'Not yet,' Lucy said. 'Not in so many words.'

'Remind me to tell you, then, when I've got time,' Barney said, and kissed her.

It would be very long before he would have time to do much in the way of talking.